Terror from the Throne

Barbara Cartland

Terror
from the
Throne

Thorndike Press • Chivers Press
Waterville, Maine USA Bath, England

This Large Print edition is published by Thorndike Press®, USA and by Chivers Press, England.

Published in 2003 in the U.S. by arrangement with International Book Marketing Limited.

Published in 2003 in the U.K. by arrangement with Cartland Promotions.

U.S. Softcover 0-7862-5220-0 (Paperback Series)
U.K. Hardcover 0-7540-7208-8 (Chivers Large Print)
U.K. Softcover 0-7540-7209-6 (Camden Large Print)

The text of this Large Print edition is unabridged.
Other aspects of the book may vary from the original edition.

Set in 16 pt. Plantin by Myrna S. Raven.

Printed in the United States on permanent paper.

British Library Cataloguing-in-Publication Data available

Library of Congress Cataloging-in-Publication Data

Cartland, Barbara, 1902–
    Terror from the throne / Barbara Cartland.
        p. cm.
    ISBN 0-7862-5220-0 (lg. print : sc : alk. paper)
    1. Kings and rulers — Fiction.   2. Large type books.
I. Title.
PR6005.A765T46 2003
    823′.912—dc21   2003041333

Terror
from the
Throne

Author's Note

Cocaine comes from an evergreen shrub, *Erythroxylum coca,* which flourishes in Western South America and in some regions of the Far East.

The active alkaloid can be absorbed systematically by chewing the leaves, smoking, imbibing or infusion, or taking the pure, extracted principle as snuff or by injection.

Nowadays, cocaine has very few medical indications, these being confined to its employment as a local surface anaesthetic.

It has now been supplanted, more or less, by synthetic analogues.

It behaves as a stimulant on the body generally and on the brain specifically, giving rise to excitement and pleasure.

Appetite is blunted and the onset of fatigue is delayed, only to be followed by reactionary exhaustion.

There is an urge to take a further dose to maintain the lifting of spirits and energy, and thus addiction begins.

chapter one

1896

"It is no use," Queen Victoria said, "I cannot give what I do not possess. There is no Princess of the Royal Family available."

She spoke sharply.

It annoyed her when she was asked to place one of her relatives on a throne in Europe and there was no one obtainable.

The Prime Minister, the Marquess of Salisbury, gave a sigh while the Earl of Rosebery, Secretary of State for Foreign Affairs, frowned.

After an uncomfortable silence the Marquess said:

"I know Your Majesty understands better than anybody else how important it is that we keep the Balkan States, even the smallest of them, from coming under the influence of Russia."

The Queen was well aware that it was not merely a question of influence.

The truth was that the Russians were doing everything they could to make trouble in the Balkans.

They were, in fact, inciting a revolution.

There was another awkward silence until the Earl of Rosebery said somewhat tentatively:

"I have a suggestion, Ma'am, but I am not at all sure that Your Majesty will like it."

"What is it?" the Queen asked.

She was always awe-inspiring, but never more than when she was annoyed with her Statesmen and at a loss diplomatically.

"I was just thinking, Ma'am," the Earl explained, "that Princess Beatrice of Leros has a daughter who is now grown up."

The Queen stared at him.

"Princess Beatrice?" she queried.

"You will remember, Ma'am," the Earl continued, "that when Her Royal Highness came to England after the assassination of her husband, Prince Philimon, Your Majesty was gracious enough to give the Princess and her daughter a Grace and Favour house at Hampton Court Palace."

"That was a long time ago," the Queen said, "and I suppose I must be honest in saying I had forgotten about her."

"Princess Beatrice," the Marquess of Salisbury interrupted, "is only distantly related to Your Majesty. In fact, she did not rank as Royalty until Prince Philimon came to England, fell in love with her, and they were married despite certain protests from the Greek Government."

"I do recall something about it now," the Queen admitted, "but as you say, Prime Minister, The Princess Beatrice is only distantly related to me."

"At the same time," the Prime Minister replied, "when she married Prince Philimon she became definitely a member of the Greek Royal Family."

"Yes, yes, of course," the Queen agreed.

She spoke in a rather irritated manner because it annoyed her that she had not remembered the Princess herself.

Also, she thought the Marquess of Salisbury was being somewhat didactic.

"Unless I am mistaken, Ma'am," the Earl of Rosebery said quietly, "the Princess's daughter was named after Your Majesty and is now at least eighteen."

The Queen drew a deep breath.

The two Statesmen waited somewhat apprehensively. They knew it had always annoyed her when minor Royalty christened their children with her name.

As they were inevitably grateful to her for arranging their marriage, they thought they were paying her a compliment.

At the moment she had over twenty

members of her family seated on various thrones of Europe.

Although she had protested over and over again in private to the Prime Minister and the Secretary of State for Foreign Affairs that she had no wish for there to be any "Queen Victoria" on a throne except herself.

As if he suddenly remembered this, the Earl of Rosebery said hastily:

"I believe that Princess Beatrice's daughter has always been called Toria, since the English found her other name, which is Aleris, difficult to pronounce."

The Queen's eyes lost a little of their irritation before she replied:

"I suppose, in the circumstances, unless we tell King Inged that we cannot help him, we must consider Prince Philimon's daughter, Aleris."

The Prime Minister drew in his breath.

"That would be very gracious of Your Majesty," the Marquess said quietly, "and since I am sure you would, Ma'am, like to inspect Princess Aleris, I will send a messenger to Hampton Court Palace immediately."

There was a pause before the Queen said:

"I seem to know very little about King

Inged. Has he ever visited England?"

"No, Ma'am," the Earl of Rosebery replied. "Actually there is nothing about him in my files except some recent reports that the Russians are doing their usual trick of infiltrating into his Kingdom. That, of course, is why he is seeking the protection of Your Majesty by taking an English Bride."

When it was known that a small Monarchy or Principality of Europe was under the protection of Great Britain, those planning to encroach on it were warned to take care.

Politically, as the two Marquesses knew only too well, a great number of these small Kingdoms were in danger.

The Russians were infiltrating wherever they could into the Balkans.

The Queen insisted on being informed of every move that took place.

She knew, even better than her Statesmen did, the value of a country which, however small, could fly, as well as their own flag, the Union Jack.

Every available Princess of the Royal blood had been married off into various European Kingdoms.

Some were so small and obscure that they occupied little space on the map.

At the same time, under the shelter of Britain they acquired an importance they had never had before.

"Very well," the Queen said to the Prime Minister. "Send Princess Beatrice and her daughter a message that I wish to see them here as soon as possible."

She looked towards the Earl of Rosebery as she said:

"I would like more information about Klaklov and about the King. It seems extraordinary that he has never communicated with me before."

"I will see to it immediately, Ma'am," the Earl replied.

The two Statesmen rose to their feet, kissed the Queen's hand, then backed slowly and with dignity from the room.

Only when the door had been closed behind them did the Earl of Rosebery give a deep sigh.

"That should solve one problem at any rate," he said.

The Prime Minister laughed.

"I would have bet a large sum against our pulling that one off!"

"It was only by the 'skin of our teeth,'" the Earl remarked, "and although I hope the Queen has forgotten her animosity towards Prince Philimon, I would not mind

14

betting that she remembers every detail of it."

"Of course she does," the Marquess agreed. "One can never fault her on history where it concerns her own family."

"I thought for one moment," the Earl said, "that she was going to deny that Princess Beatrice is a relation."

"But she definitely is a remote one," the Marquess remarked, "and as you well know, if you probe back far enough, we are all of us related to Adam!"

The Earl laughed and the sound seemed to echo round the rather dismal corridors of Windsor Castle.

Built originally as a fortification, the Castle never seemed to lose its rather formidable atmosphere.

Outside in the court-yard the carriage which was to take the two Statesmen back to London was waiting.

They got into it.

As the horses rode off they were both thinking that the audience with Her Majesty, which had been a somewhat tricky one, had gone off better than they had dared hope.

That evening Princess Beatrice was astonished to receive a letter from the Secretary of State for Foreign Affairs.

It informed her that she and her daughter were to proceed to Windsor Castle the following day at the direct command of Her Majesty Queen Victoria.

A carriage would be sent for them soon after breakfast, and if it was possible, the Earl of Rosebery himself would come in person to escort them to the Castle.

The Princess read it over in the small, rather constricting Grace and Favour house she had been given in the precincts of Hampton Court Palace.

She stared at the communication in astonishment.

In the ten years she had been in England after her husband's death, she had not had one single communication from the Queen.

It was not surprising.

The Queen had tried to direct Prince Philimon on how he should handle the comparatively small Greek island over which he ruled.

He had graciously been permitted to marry an Englishwoman who was distantly related to the Queen.

Consequently, Her Majesty had thought it her right to tell him how to run his own domain.

He was over thirty at the time and had very decided ideas of his own.

He therefore resented her interference.

He had told her, not particularly tactfully, more or less to mind her own business.

The Queen had been furious.

When two years later the Prince was assassinated, the Secretary of State for Foreign Affairs had found it hard to persuade the Queen to write a letter of condolence to his widow.

Her Majesty did not welcome Princess Beatrice when she returned to England.

She had come to save not only her own life but also that of her daughter.

The Queen would not receive her, and it was with the greatest difficulty that the Prime Minister managed to persuade her to give Princess Beatrice a Grace and Favour house.

"Her Royal Highness has no money, Your Majesty," he said persistently.

"That is hardly my fault!" the Queen retorted sharply.

There was an uncomfortable silence until the Secretary of State for Foreign Affairs, who was also present, said:

"I cannot believe that Your Majesty would think it advisable for a Royal Princess to have to accept charity. That is what Her Royal Highness will be obliged to do if she is left as destitute as she is at this moment."

"And what has happened to her family?" the Queen asked.

"With the exception of Your Majesty," the Prime Minister answered somewhat daringly, "they are either dead, or else so poor that they can only just look after themselves, and have no room in their houses, or in their lives, for the Princess and her daughter."

Finally the Queen had capitulated.

Princess Beatrice was allotted the smallest and the least desirable of the Grace and Favour houses at Hampton Court Palace.

There was also a grant of money so small that the Foreign Secretary thought it was almost an insult.

However, the Princess was extremely grateful.

Because he was a kindly man, later he enquired after her.

He found that she was managing by selling her needlework, at which she was extremely proficient.

In this way she was able to provide for herself and the education of her daughter.

It was ironic that the child had been christened Victoria when she was born.

This was because Prince Philimon had been grateful at that moment to the Queen for allowing him to marry the woman he loved.

Her Majesty had not yet taken it upon herself to instruct him to manage his own domain.

Prince Philimon, however, soon realised that he had made a mistake.

He could not change the name with which his daughter had been christened.

Yet it could be abbreviated, and she was always called "Toria."

Prince Beatrice, as she finished reading the letter from Lord Rosebery, called:

"Toria! Toria!"

Her voice seemed to echo round the small house, and from upstairs her daughter replied:

"Coming, Mama."

A few seconds later, Toria ran through the open door of the Sitting-Room.

Her mother was standing by the window.

She was holding in her hand the unexpected letter which she was reading again.

"What is it, Mama? What has happened?" Toria asked as she came towards her.

Princess Beatrice handed her daughter the letter, saying:

"I do not really know what this means, Toria, I am too frightened to guess."

With a puzzled expression Toria took the letter from her mother and read it.

As she did so, Princess Beatrice looked at her daughter as if for the first time.

Toria was very lovely.

She had been clever enough when she was born to inherit the classical Greek features of her Father.

Her eyes were a deep sea-blue like her Mother's.

Her hair resembled that of neither parent.

It was the gold of the dawn, the tips touched with red, as if from the warmth of the sun.

Her complexion was fair.

In fact, it might have been the "peaches and cream" of any English beauty.

But Toria had also inherited the long, dark lashes which were characteristic of her Greek Father.

Altogether she was beautiful in a very unusual way.

Because they were so poor and unimportant, Princess Beatrice had worried about her daughter.

Now that Toria was grown up, how, she asked herself, would she ever meet the right sort of men, who one day, she prayed, would include a husband?

The other residents of the Grace and Favour houses at Hampton Court Palace were very kind to Princess Beatrice and Toria.

They were, however, all very old.

Generally, those who lived in the shadow of the great Palace were forgotten by the world outside.

Now — Princess Beatrice could hardly believe it — this letter had arrived, commanding them to appear at Windsor Castle.

She could think of only one reason for it, and that she did not dare to put into words.

Toria finished reading the letter.

"We have been invited to the Castle, Mama!" she declared in amazement. "What can have happened to make the Queen take notice of us now, after being so disagreeable?"

"Oh, do be careful, Darling! Do not speak like that!" the Princess begged. "As you know, the Queen has never forgiven your Father for standing up to her. That is why all the years we have been here she has never acknowledged our existence."

There was not a bitter note in Princess Beatrice's voice.

It was one of sadness!

After the Queen recovered a little from the loss of her beloved Prince Albert, the Princess had hoped, indeed prayed, that Toria would be invited to some of the functions that took place at the Castle.

But the years came and went.

They had to create their own small festivities with the people around them.

It meant that Toria never went to a party where there were young people.

She had never been to a Ball.

More important, she had never been presented to the Queen as a *débutante*.

Now, out of the blue, this letter had come.

The Princess did not know what to make of it.

Unless — and now her heart almost stopped beating at the thought — the Queen intended to marry Toria off as she had done with so many of her relatives.

The residents of the Grace and Favour houses had no direct communication with Buckingham Palace, Windsor Castle, or Marlborough House.

Yet, by some magical means of their

own, they knew exactly what was going on.

They talked to Princess Beatrice of the Queen's gradual emergence from the dark days of her mourning for Prince Albert.

They discussed the Drawing-Rooms that took place at Buckingham Palace.

They gossiped about the Prince of Wales and Princess Alexandra, who frequently deputised for the Queen.

They also chatted, but in very low voices, about the love-affairs of the Prince of Wales.

His infatuations for one Beauty after another, which had started with the actress Mrs. Lily Langtry, lost nothing in the telling.

Toria, of course, had not been permitted to listen to these conversations.

As it happened, she was not particularly interested.

Her Mother had arranged that she should have a number of extra lessons.

Unlike most girls her age, she found them entrancingly interesting.

The elderly widow of one of England's most successful Ambassadors to France taught her French.

The Ambassador had married a Frenchwoman, but she had, surprisingly, preferred to stay in England rather than return to her own country.

She enjoyed having Toria as a pupil.

She refused, although the Princess protested, to accept any remuneration for it.

Toria learnt from her perfect Parisian French.

She also learnt to cook in the French fashion because the ex-Ambassadress could not find a local woman to employ who would attempt French *cuisine*.

The Princess was insistent also that Toria should not forget the Greek she had spoken with her Father.

There was, fortunately, amongst the strangely varied inhabitants of the Grace and Favour houses, a very old Diplomat who had spent many years in Greece.

He had also been posted in Austria and he therefore was able to teach Toria both Greek and German.

He added, because she was curious, a smattering of Russian.

She had thus become proficient in several different languages.

Any additional language, therefore, was easy for her to acquire, especially those of Balkan countries.

The Diplomat told her how he had managed when he was young to move from country to country and in a few days to understand the natives.

"It is what I would like to do myself," Toria sighed.

"You will have to find yourself a husband who is a Diplomat," he answered. "Think how useful you will be to him!"

Toria had laughed.

Yet, as she walked back to her own house she often thought her world was a very small one.

If it had not been for the Palace and the interesting people, even if they were old, who lived in the shadow of it, she would have found it constricting.

As it was, she went from house to house and they all welcomed her as if she were a visiting Angel.

She was an exceptionally sympathetic listener.

They therefore told her of their past, of the places where they had lived, also of the frightening situations they had encountered as well as the more pleasant ones.

"It is like having somebody enacting a Play in front of me," Toria had said once to her mother.

"I am glad you feel like that, Darling," the Princess replied. "You are so like your Father. He used to come to me and say: 'I met the most interesting man to-day, and

— what do you think, Darling? — he has been to Tibet, where I would love to go.' He described it so vividly that I felt I might almost have been with him as he journeyed over mountains and dangerous passes to reach Lhasa."

"That is what I would like to do," Toria had replied.

Apart from all this, of course, there was Hampton Court Palace itself.

It was Queen Victoria who had been brave enough in the face of opposition to open the Palace to the public.

To Toria it was a joy beyond words to wander from room to room, remembering the history that had taken place there.

She felt as if she relived every drama connected with it that she had read about.

It was a better education, Princess Beatrice thought, than she could ever have had from a Governess, or even from one of the Schools for Young Ladies which had become fashionable.

Toria talked to the Curator and the Librarian, and read the History Books.

She felt that she herself was one of the ghosts that haunted the Palace.

Now, as she finished reading the letter, she said excitedly:

"At last I am to meet the Queen! We

have talked about her for so long, and they say she is terrifying!"

"I cannot imagine why she wishes to see us after all this time," Princess Beatrice said.

"Perhaps her conscience is pricking her," Toria suggested, "or else she is going to tell us that she wants our little house for somebody else!"

Princess Beatrice gave a cry of horror.

"I never thought of that! Oh, Toria, what shall we do if she turns us out?"

"I was only teasing, Mama," Toria said. "I am sure the Queen cannot be as cruel as that, even though they say that strong men tremble at the thought of entering her presence, and the Prince of Wales is terrified of her!"

"You should not listen to such gossip!" the Princess murmured.

"It is all we have to listen to!" Toria replied. "You know, Mama, there is nothing that excites all our friends here more than hearing who is the latest 'Charmer' who has bewitched the Prince of Wales!"

Princess Beatrice gave a cry of horror.

"Toria, you are not to say such things! Supposing the Queen heard you?"

Toria laughed.

"She is not likely to do that! We have

lived here for ten years, Mama, and she has never so much as sent us a message of goodwill at Christmas!"

Princess Beatrice knew this was true.

But because it was a subject she did not wish to pursue, she merely said:

"What shall we wear? Oh, Toria, we must look our best!"

Because they had so little money, the Princess made all their clothes and did so extremely skilfully.

However, they were all sensible garments because material was expensive.

She could not help thinking they would both appear very dowdy compared to other Ladies in the Castle.

The next morning Princess Beatrice and Toria were dressed and waiting long before the carriage was due to arrive.

The Princess knew that anything Toria wore was transformed simply by her wearing it.

Nothing could be plainer than her navy-blue gown with its small jacket that had a little braid round the collar.

But it did not disguise Toria's tiny waist nor the soft curves of her figure and the grace with which she walked.

The hat she wore was also quite plain,

but it haloed her sun-touched hair.

Because she was excited, her eyes seemed to fill her small, pointed face and sparkled like stars.

They drove away from Hampton Court Palace in a very comfortable carriage drawn by two white horses.

The coachman had brought with him a note from the Earl of Rosebery apologising for being unable to escort them personally.

"At least we are arriving in grandeur!" Toria declared.

It was quite a long drive to Windsor Castle, but Toria enjoyed every moment of it.

She looked out the window, exclaiming at everything she saw.

"Look, Mama, look at all those people shopping in this narrow street!"

There was a man playing the violin with a dog sitting at his feet.

"He is guarding the money being thrown into his master's hat by the passers-by," Toria explained.

Everything they saw was an excitement.

When finally they arrived at the Castle, Toria could only wonder at how impressive and formidable it looked.

As the horses came to a standstill, she realised that her Mother had been very quiet all the way.

Princess Beatrice was in fact quite frightened of meeting the Queen.

"Cheer up, Mama!" she urged. "After all, she cannot eat us, and unless we say something stupid, we shall have the fun of the drive back!"

Princess Beatrice forced a smile.

However, as they entered through the heavy oak door into the hall of Windsor Castle with its high ceiling, Toria was aware that her Mother was praying.

A young and handsome *Aide-de-Camp* was waiting to escort them.

Toria had met very few young men.

Yet she was intelligent enough to realise that he looked at her, first with surprise, then with an unmistakeable admiration.

"I believe this is your first visit to the Castle," he said.

"Our very first!" Toria replied. "And because I have never been here before, but have heard so much about it, I was beginning to think it was just a myth!"

The *Aide-de-Camp* laughed.

"I assure you it is very solid and will not vanish, if that is what is worrying you."

"I hope not! At least, not until I have seen all of it!"

He laughed again.

He pointed out particular items of interest as they walked down the long, twisting corridors.

At last they came to the Queen's private apartments.

It was then the Earl of Rosebery, who had been waiting for them, appeared.

He apologised to Princess Beatrice for having been unable to escort them to Windsor as he had intended.

"I am sure Your Royal Highness will understand that in my position I never know from one moment to another what will occur and, however much I regret it, I cannot be in two places at once."

The Princess smiled.

Toria thought that the Foreign Secretary was being very diplomatic.

'He understands that Mama is frightened,' she thought, 'and now he has put her at her ease.'

They talked for a short while, Lord Rosebery making himself charming to the Princess.

His attentions had brought a slight flush to her cheeks.

She looked very much happier and more relaxed than when they had first arrived.

Then there was the summons for which they were waiting, and the *Aide-de-Camp* preceded them to the door.

As it opened, Toria thought from the way they were all behaving that she might be in a Church rather than entering a Drawing-Room.

But one glance showed her that the Queen's Sitting-Room was very personal.

Never had Toria seen such a profusion of photographs in silver frames.

There were aspidistras, antimacassars, and small tables crowded with assorted ornaments.

Then at the far end there was the Queen.

She was not, as Toria had expected, sitting on a golden throne and wearing a crown.

She was just a small elderly woman dressed in the deepest black.

chapter two

"I will call on Your Royal Highness to-morrow," Lord Rosebery said, "and bring with me the Minister from Klaklov."

"We shall look forward to seeing you," Princess Beatrice replied.

Lord Rosebery stood back, a footman closed the carriage-door, and the horses moved off.

There was silence as they turned out of the great gate-way and started down the hill.

Toria was looking out the window with unseeing eyes.

Her Mother glanced at her.

Then somewhat nervously she said:

"It was a great surprise, Dearest!"

"I have no wish to marry King Inged," Toria said.

Her voice was firm.

For a moment it seemed to ring out in the closeness of the carriage.

"I know it is something of a shock," Princess Beatrice replied. "At the same time, my Darling, you will be a Queen!"

Toria did not answer.

She was still feeling, as she had when the Queen told her why they had been sent for, that the ceiling had fallen down on her head.

How could it be possible?

How could she believe for a moment that she was to marry a man she had never seen and travel a very long way to meet him?

Queen Victoria had made it quite clear that it was a privilege and an honour for her to be the Queen of Klaklov.

Moreover, she would further the interests of the British Empire by giving that country stability.

The Queen had dwelt lightly on the Russian menace in the Balkans.

As it happened, Toria was already aware of this.

Her discussions with the old Diplomat who had taught her languages had kept her up to date with what was taking place in Europe.

She knew that Russia had designs to encroach on India and that it was already exercising a great deal of pressure on the Balkans. That was a subject which concerned the Diplomat profoundly.

Because he had few friends of his own age to talk to, he talked to Toria.

As she was so interested, she listened intently.

But never in her wildest dreams had she thought it possible that she would be sent away from her Mother and England and that she would live in a small country which was, in fact, quite difficult to find on the map.

She knew, however, that Klaklov lay on the North coast of the Aegean Sea on the Eastern border of Macedonia and opposite the island of Thasos.

This, she realised, made it important to the Russians, who had always sought an outlet to the Aegean for their ships.

But History and Geography were one thing — marriage was another.

She remembered how her Father had fallen in love with her Mother.

She had always imagined in her dreams that somehow she would meet a man and get to know him well before there was any talk of her being his wife.

Now she had been informed by the Queen that she was to travel to Klaklov.

She would be married, on her arrival, to the King, and the sooner the ceremony took place, the better.

Toria had been too astonished to say anything.

It was, in fact, the Queen who had done all the talking.

"Because I understand your financial

position," she said to Princess Beatrice, "I will provide as a wedding-gift your daughter's trousseau, but you understand that as she is to leave within a fortnight, there will not be time to have many gowns made specially for her."

"It . . . is very . . . g-gracious of Your . . . M-Majesty," Princess Beatrice had stammered.

Toria remained silent.

She was well aware that the Queen was forcing her into an acceptance of the situation.

Although it seemed unlikely, Her Majesty was being more pleasant than she would have been if the situation had not been urgent.

Toria was certain that it was a diplomatic move.

The Queen was therefore carrying it out at the request, not only of King Inged, but also of Lord Rosebery.

The Secretary of State for Foreign Affairs was very affable when they left the Royal presence.

He had been called in after the Queen had told Princess Beatrice and Toria what was to be done.

He made his congratulations sound both effusive and sincere.

"I have arranged," the Queen said, "for Princess Beatrice's daughter to marry King Inged and, as His Majesty's Ministers have requested, the Bride will proceed to Klaklov in two weeks time."

Lord Rosebery had bowed in obeisance.

At the same time, Toria was well aware that he was not only delighted, but relieved at the information.

Nobody had asked her opinion: her acceptance had been taken for granted.

She had hardly spoken one word before they were dismissed.

Lord Rosebery took them quickly down the corridors to where in the court-yard the carriage was waiting for them.

Now, as the horses conveyed them, Toria felt as if her brain was beginning to work again.

She could think more clearly.

"There must be a reason for all this haste," she said at length.

"You heard what Her Majesty said," her mother replied. "There is a certain amount of tension all over the Balkans, and the King's Ministers have pleaded for an English Queen who will protect them against any unwelcome interference from their neighbours."

"The Russians!" Toria said beneath her breath.

"Of course it will be a rush to collect your trousseau," the Princess was saying, "but that is a familiar experience for every Court Dressmaker, and as the Queen is paying, they will be only too willing to work overtime."

She paused before she said in a different tone:

"Oh, Darling, it will be so wonderful for you to have beautiful gowns from the best Dressmakers in London rather than those I make for you."

Toria was not listening.

She was thinking that very little had been said about the King himself.

She had no idea if he was young or old, nor had anything been said about his antecedents.

Suddenly she thought of the one person who was likely to know about him!

She resolved to visit the old Diplomat at the earliest opportunity.

Her Mother was so delighted that at last she had received some recognition from Queen Victoria.

And incredibly, Toria would be a reigning Queen.

Only when they reached their own tiny house did Toria feel that the journey to Windsor Castle and back could not have been real.

It was just a figment of her imagination.

It seemed extraordinary that it had all taken place so quickly.

It passed through her mind that the Queen might have been gracious enough to invite them to stay to luncheon.

However, they were only a little late for their meagre meal.

Princess Beatrice hurried into the kitchen to announce their return.

Toria went up to her bedroom to take off her hat and jacket.

The small room had all her favourite books arranged on shelves along one wall.

There were small ornaments dotted about which she had been given over the years.

Now she would be leaving this tiny haven she had thought of as her own, leaving it for a Kingdom she had never seen and barely heard of.

When she went downstairs again she found her Mother already waiting and luncheon was on the table.

"What I have planned," Princess Beatrice said as Toria appeared, "is that we should go to London this afternoon. There is no time to be lost and, I do not know whether you heard, but Lord Rosebery told me as we walked to the door that a carriage and horses is to be made available to us every day for the next two weeks."

Toria looked at her Mother in surprise.

"A . . . carriage and . . . horses?" she repeated stupidly.

The Princess laughed.

"I could hardly believe my ears," she said, "and of course I accepted with delight. With all we have to do, we could not possibly manage without a convenient form of conveyance."

Toria knew that was true.

At the same time, it made her feel as if she were being swept away on a tidal wave.

The next morning they could not go to London because Lord Rosebery was calling on them in the afternoon.

It was then that Toria managed to reach her friend, the Diplomat.

He was, as usual, delighted to see her.

"I expected you yesterday," he said a little reproachfully.

"I know," Toria replied, "but we had to go to Windsor Castle to see the Queen."

The old man nodded his head.

"I heard about that, and in fact everybody here is curious to know why Her

Majesty should have sent for you so unexpectedly."

Toria was aware that the sight of a Royal carriage outside their small house would be enough to start the inhabitants of the Grace and Favour apartments talking.

She was only surprised they were not aware of everything that had taken place at Windsor Castle.

"I imagine Her Majesty has found you a throne to occupy!" the old man said before she could speak.

Toria stared at him.

"How did you know that?"

He shrugged his shoulders and made a gesture with his hand that was very expressive.

"I was calculating," he said, "that there are too few Princesses left on whose head the Queen can place a crown."

Toria laughed.

"You are quite right, and I have come to ask you to tell me everything you know about Klaklov."

The old Diplomat stiffened.

"Klaklov?" he exclaimed. "You are to marry its King?"

Toria nodded.

"It never crossed my mind it would be him!" the old man said. "But of course, now I come to think of it, that tiny Kingdom would prove a tasty morsel for the Russian Eagle!"

Toria sat down in the nearest chair.

"Tell me about the King," she begged.

"I hardly dare confess it," the Diplomat said, "but Klaklov is one of the few places to which I have never been, and, to be honest, I know very little about the ruling."

"How can you disappoint me?" Toria complained. "I was relying on you to give me all the information I want about the country and the man I am . . . being *forced* to marry."

The way she said "forced" made the Diplomat look at her sharply.

"It is something you do not want?" he asked.

"Of course I do not want it!" Toria replied. "How could anyone want to marry a man they have never seen and who requires a wife only because she comes wrapped in the Union Jack!"

The Diplomat laughed gently.

"My poor child — this is the penalty you have to pay for being Royal, and, however difficult it may seem, there are compensations."

"And what are they?" Toria asked doubtfully.

His old eyes went towards the window.

"You are young and very beautiful," he said. "I have often asked myself what is to become of you living here. Most of the residents, as you know, come here to die."

Toria put out her hand and laid it gently on his arm.

"I have been very happy here," she said, "and it has always been a joy to come and visit you."

"That is the kindest thing you could have said to me," he said as he smiled. "At the same time, dear child, there is a great deal going on in the world outside. That is where you belong, not in this small graveyard!"

There was silence for a moment. Then Toria said:

"I . . . I am . . . frightened."

"Of course you are," he replied, "but life, whether it is good or bad, is always exciting and, because you are very intelligent as well as lovely, you will not only survive, but make your life as you want it to be."

"H-how can you be . . . sure of . . . that?" Toria asked.

"I know you possess courage," the old man said, "and courage is what turns the very worst things that happen into an adventure rather than a disaster!"

"B-but suppose," Toria said hesitatingly,

"the marriage *is* a disaster . . . what then?"

"There is no reason why it should be," the Diplomat answered, "but if it is, you will survive, and remember, you can always escape from a situation, however difficult, if you use your brain and follow your heart."

He looked at Toria affectionately before he said:

"You are very beautiful, my child, and you will always find there are men who will fight for you and protect you. Although what you have to do may seem for the moment frightening, it is, I assure you, far better than that you should stay here, wasting your beauty and brains on old men like myself!"

Because he spoke with a twinkle in his eyes, Toria laughed.

They sat down after that to look at the map and see exactly where Klaklov was.

Although the Diplomat could not tell her very much about the country, he had visited Greece and several parts of Macedonia.

He also had a good knowledge of the language that was spoken in Klaklov.

What he said made everything seem much more simple.

When Toria left him to go to luncheon,

she was not so fearful of the future as she had been before.

Princess Beatrice was talking of the clothes she would need.

She had made a list of everything they must purchase when they went to London the following day.

Then at half after two o'clock precisely Lord Rosebery arrived with the Minister from Klaklov.

A middle-aged man, Toria discovered that he was the Deputy Prime Minister, obviously a man of some considerable importance in his country.

He had been charged with the task of begging Queen Victoria to assist the Government by providing his country with an English Queen.

He was delighted at his success.

Toria felt as if he looked her over rather as if she were a horse whose points he appreciated.

Then he made her a long speech assuring her of the welcome she would receive when she reached Klaklov.

She realised he was eager to please.

At the same time, of the two men, she much preferred Lord Rosebery.

It was the Diplomat who had told her what a remarkable man he was.

"He is a great aristocrat," he had said, "a scholar, a millionaire, a collector of discrimination, and I can assure you he is an outstanding Foreign Secretary!"

Toria listened with interest to all he had to say.

She thought Lord Rosebery was presenting the Minister from Klaklov as if he were a puppet on a string.

"His Excellency," he said to Princess Beatrice, "has everything planned for the journey. You and the Princess will travel in a private Drawing-Room attached to the Express train as far as Naples."

He stopped to smile at her, then continued:

"There you will find waiting a Klaklovan battleship which will carry you across the Mediterranean and up the Aegean Sea to Klaklov. You will find that a far more pleasant journey than if you go all the way by rail."

Princess Beatrice smiled her appreciation, and Lord Rosebery continued:

"His Excellency will of course escort you and Baroness Giocada, who will act as Lady-in-Waiting to Princess Toria. There will also be a lady's-maid and an *Aide-de-Camp.*"

"That is very kind," Princess Beatrice replied.

"I can assure you," Lord Rosebery went on, "that everything will be done to make your journey comfortable, so that you both arrive without feeling too tired."

He was certainly being very considerate, Toria thought.

When at last it was possible for her to speak, she asked:

"Can you tell me a little about the King himself?"

There was, she thought, a moment's silence, as if Lord Rosebery were thinking quickly.

At last he said:

"I can only apologise, Princess, that His Excellency was unable to bring with him a portrait of King Inged, but when I met him some years ago I thought him a very good-looking man."

"H-how old is he?" Toria enquired.

She knew as she spoke that her Mother was looking at her nervously.

Toria was aware that again Lord Rosebery hesitated and looked at the Minister as if for guidance.

In a slightly broken accent His Excellency replied in English:

"His Majesty is getting on towards middle-age. At the same time, he is young at heart, and I am sure, Princess, you will find the Palace very beautiful, especially the gardens."

He then began describing the contents of the Palace — the fine pictures, the Greek statues, and the very fine views that could be seen from the windows.

By the time he had finished, Lord Rosebery was ready to return to London.

Addressing Princess Beatrice, he told her that she had only to ask for anything she required for it to be supplied immediately.

He finished by saying:

"Her Majesty informed me after you had left how much she had enjoyed meeting Your Royal Highness again, and that she was in fact delighted with Princess Toria."

He then rose to his feet and started to move towards the door.

Although Toria had many more questions to ask the Minister from Klaklov, it was now impossible for her to do so.

Only as their visitors drove away did she say to her Mother:

"They are certainly being very secretive about the King! Do you suppose he is deformed in some way, or so old that he is in a wheel-chair?"

Princess Beatrice gave a little cry of horror.

"How can you think such things, Toria?

You heard the Minister say he has not yet reached middle-age. That means he is only in his late thirties."

"The Minister did not say so," Toria persisted, "and I cannot help thinking they are being somewhat mysterious about him."

"You are just imagining things," Princess Beatrice replied. "Although I agree that you should have been shown a portrait of him —"

"At the same time," Toria interrupted, "why did he not come himself to ask Her Majesty for a Bride? Then he could have chosen a wife for himself."

Princess Beatrice sighed.

"That sounds reasonable, but you know as well as I do that if the Queen refused to help him, it would have been a personal insult to the King, while to refuse the Minister would be merely a diplomatic rebuff."

She saw that her daughter was unimpressed, and put her arms round her.

"I know it is all very worrying, Darling," she said, "but I learnt when I was reigning with Papa in Leros that a diplomatic move means endless talk, and with people you are not concerned with personally. It is something which, in the future, you will have to accept."

"I . . . suppose so," Toria replied doubtfully. "At the same time, it seems to me to be a very high-handed way of going about things."

"He is a King," Princess Beatrice pointed out, "and Kings, however small their Kingdoms, consider themselves of very great importance!"

"And yet they have to crawl to Queen Victoria when they want a wife!" Toria retorted. "You would think a King would have enough initiative to find one for himself!"

"If you talk like that, you will get us into a great deal of trouble!" Princess Beatrice admonished her daughter. "When we next see Lord Rosebery, we will ask him to provide us with more details about the King and his country."

"I certainly know nothing about either at the moment!" Toria said.

She did not wait for her Mother to reply.

Putting on her hat, she hurried to the house of the Diplomat to tell him what had occurred.

All too quickly the days passed as they bought Toria's trousseau.

Although she tried to tell herself that what she wore was immaterial and it was what she was going to do that mattered, she could not help being thrilled.

It was exciting to have the most expensive and exclusive Dressmakers pleading with her to accept this gown or that.

It was hard to believe that she could decide regardless of the price.

There was no time to have anything made except the wedding-gown and two gowns for formal occasions.

Therefore, she and Princess Beatrice went from shop to shop.

Toria had an exquisite figure, but she was very slim.

Nearly everything she tried on had to be taken in if it was to fit her.

Some of the gowns, however lavish, looked grotesque because they were much too large.

Gradually the trousseau grew and grew.

Finally Princess Beatrice was afraid that the Queen would be angry at their extravagance.

"Do not worry, Mama," Toria begged. "She told us we could have whatever we wanted and could get in two weeks, and if what we wanted is half Bond Street, Her Majesty should not complain."

It would be warm when they arrived in Klaklov.

Yet Princess Beatrice was wise enough to

choose a few coats which would be suitable later on in the year.

"At least the King should not have to spend any money on me for some time," Toria said, "and as we do not know whether he is generous or mean, I am glad I shall not have to ask him for a new hat!"

"You look lovely, Darling, in everything we have bought," her Mother replied.

She was insistent on Toria wearing soft pastel colours.

They made a perfect frame for her fair hair and translucent skin.

Several of the gowns were white.

Her wedding-gown was of chiffon and white satin, embroidered with diamanté which sparkled as Toria moved.

"You look like a Fairy Princess!" her Mother said when it was finished.

Toria stood in front of the long mirror in which she could see herself completely.

When she had a diamond tiara on her head, or perhaps a crown, besides a flowing wedding veil, she would look as if she had stepped out of a picture-book.

She could not help feeling, however, that it would have been consoling to know what the man standing beside her would look like.

Would he be the Prince Charming of her dreams?

Of course she had dreamt that some day she would marry somebody she loved and who loved her.

They would then live happily ever after.

She had been acutely aware of her Father and Mother's happiness.

She would see her Father's eyes light up whenever her Mother appeared.

Whenever they were separated, even for a short time, her Mother would run to greet him on his return.

She would look as excited as a young girl.

'That is what I want to feel,' Toria thought, 'but how could the King be in love with me if he has never seen me? Perhaps, although they are too afraid to say so, he is in love with somebody of his own nationality but is unable for some reason to marry her.'

She would lie awake at night, thinking of what lay ahead.

She tried to believe that the Diplomat was right.

He had said that however difficult her future life might be, it was better than staying at Hampton Court Palace with people not much younger than himself to talk to.

"I am sure it will be all right," Toria told herself reassuringly.

Her Mother was delighted because she would be a Queen.

Yet she knew that she herself was secretly afraid, afraid that the King would not think of her as a woman, but merely as a protector against his enemies.

'I want to be loved,' she would wish in the darkness of her little room. 'Oh . . . please . . . God . . . whatever else I may find in Klaklov . . . please . . . let me find . . . love!'

chapter three

As the Express train gathered speed across France, Toria thought she must be dreaming.

Nothing had seemed real since she had been summoned to Windsor Castle, but two days ago the dream had become a nightmare.

Princess Beatrice had finished packing one of her cases which contained hats and bonnets.

"That is finished," she said with satisfaction. "But I think, Dearest, when you arrive in Klaklov, they will think you have brought all of Bond Street with you."

"It is very nearly the truth," Toria laughed.

Her Mother stood up, and, bending down, picked up the large hat-box.

Then she gave a scream and Toria looked at her in astonishment.

"What is the matter, Mama?"

"It is my back," Princess Beatrice gasped.

She sat down on the side of the bed.

Toria realised that she looked very pale,

as if she were going to faint.

"What has happened? How can you have hurt yourself?" she asked.

"I do not know," Princess Beatrice replied, "but my back is agony."

Frightened at what had happened, Toria sent the carriage, which fortunately was waiting outside, to fetch the Queen's Doctor, Sir James Reid, from Windsor.

She then helped her Mother into bed.

Although Princess Beatrice did not protest, she had no wish to lie down.

"I am sure that is what you must do, Mama," Toria insisted.

She had been right.

When Sir James Reid came, he had diagnosed that Princess Beatrice had slipped a disc in her spine.

When Toria was alone with him she asked what it meant.

"To explain it in very simple language," Sir James replied, "we all of us have a small bit of soft material between each of the vertebrae in our spine. If this gets misplaced, then one suffers a most unpleasant pain until it grows again."

Toria looked at him apprehensively.

"How long does that take?"

"I am afraid Her Royal Highness will have to lie on her back for six weeks,"

Sir James answered.

Toria gave a little cry.

"Then would you be kind enough to inform Lord Rosebery that I cannot leave Mama and go to Klaklov."

Sir James drove back to Windsor and fortunately found that Lord Rosebery was calling on the Queen on some matter of diplomatic importance.

When he heard what had occurred he came to Hampton Court immediately, even though it was late in the evening.

Because Toria knew it was important for him to understand how serious her Mother's condition was, she took him up to her bedroom.

Princess Beatrice was lying, on Sir James's instructions, flat on her back with just a very low pillow behind her head.

She tried to sit up when Toria brought Lord Rosebery into the bedroom, but gave a little murmur of pain.

"Please do not move," Lord Rosebery said. "But Your Royal Highness will understand that I have to discuss this matter with you."

"I cannot leave Mama," Toria said firmly before her Mother could reply.

Lord Rosebery sat down in a chair.

"Let me first say how deeply distressed I

am that this should have happened to you," he said to Princess Beatrice. "But I think you will understand when I say that it is impossible at this juncture to change all the plans we have made for the wedding which is to take place in Klaklov as soon as your daughter arrives."

"I have told you," Toria interposed quickly, "that I cannot possibly leave Mama. There is no-one to look after her, and therefore I have to be here."

"I can understand your feelings," Lord Rosebery said, "but at the same time I know your Mother will realise that history cannot wait for individuals, and in going to Klaklov you are making history, or, perhaps, to put it more bluntly, you are saving it."

"Then of course she must go," Princess Beatrice said a little faintly.

"What I am going to suggest," Lord Rosebery answered, "is that Your Royal Highness comes to stay with me, first at my house in London, where you can have the best medical attention."

He smiled at her and then went on:

"Then, when you are feeling better, we could move to my house in the country, where I know you will enjoy the garden, even if you still have to see it from a strange angle."

He smiled as he spoke.

"Are you really suggesting that I should come and stay with you?" she said. "I should be nothing but an encumbrance."

"I assure you," Lord Rosebery replied, "I should be delighted to have you as a guest. Since my wife died, my elder sister has been staying with me and acting as Hostess."

There was just a little tremor in his voice when he spoke of his wife.

She had died four years earlier, and everyone who knew him well was aware how deeply he missed her.

"I am sure that after a few weeks your back will not be as painful as it is at the moment," he said. "At least you will have someone to talk to and I can assure you that I shall enjoy your company."

Toria drew in her breath.

She knew it would be marvellous for her Mother to enjoy the luxury of Lord Rosebery's houses.

She would have someone as clever as she was to talk to.

She was too intelligent not to realise that if she herself was too young for the other inhabitants of the Grace and Favour houses at Hampton Court, the same applied to her Mother.

Princess Beatrice was only thirty-seven and still very beautiful.

Because they were so poor, the Princess had been too proud to accept hospitality that she could not return.

Actually invitations to anything more than a cup of tea were few and far between.

At the same time, she had no wish to go to Klaklov without her Mother.

The one thing which had made the long journey and the hurried marriage tolerable was the knowledge that her Mother would be with her.

As Lord Rosebery turned his face in her direction, Toria knew without being told that he was desperately eager for her to go on with the arrangements that had been made.

He would do everything in his power to prevent them being upset.

She had therefore agreed to do what he wished, even it if made her feel more frightened than ever of marrying a man of whom she had learnt little or nothing except that he was a King.

She found it very hard not to cry when she said good-bye to her Mother.

At the same time, the carriage had arrived containing the Minister from Klaklov and the Baroness Giocada, who was to be her Lady-in-Waiting.

Lord Rosebery arrived too.

His carriage was even grander and larger than the one that was to take her to the station.

He showed Toria how he had arranged a comfortable support for her Mother.

It stretched from the back of the carriage on to the small seat opposite.

The Princess was carried from her bed-room by Sir James and a Nurse.

Watching them, Toria realised that they were doing it so skilfully that her Mother was not suffering any pain.

Only when she was safely in the carriage did she say good-bye.

She knew that her Mother would wish her to be brave and not be emotional in front of so many strangers.

"Good-bye, my Darling," she said. "God bless you, and take care of you. I shall be thinking and praying for you every day."

Toria held her Mother close, as it was impossible for her to speak.

Then, on Lord Rosebery's orders, Princess Beatrice's carriage with the Doctor and the Nurse moved off first.

He travelled with Toria in the carriage which was conveying her to the station.

Later, when they said good-bye, he said quietly:

"I am not only grateful to you but also very proud that you are behaving so courageously in very unfortunate circumstances."

He paused before he continued:

"I am relying on you to serve England and to save Klaklov."

He spoke quietly, as he did not wish the Minister to overhear what he was saying.

Toria could only reply:

"I promise, My Lord, I will do my best."

Lord Rosebery smiled.

"And no-one can do more than that," he said.

Toria's luggage had already gone ahead with the Courier.

When she was seen off by Lord Rosebery, the Station Master, and two *Aides-de-Camp,* she knew that she had already become a person of importance.

Certainly everything was done to make her feel comfortable.

Even the sea behaved kindly when they crossed the Channel and was smooth as the proverbial Duck Pond.

As Lord Rosebery had promised, there was a Drawing-Room attached to the Express train at Calais.

This was to carry them across France to Italy.

Toria had never been in a Private Coach before.

She found it had not only a comfortable Drawing-Room which Queen Victoria enjoyed when she travelled, but three bedrooms.

The largest was for her, and she suspected it was the one that was used by the Queen.

There were two smaller ones for the Baroness and His Excellency, the Minister.

Toria's lady's-maid had to sleep on a bed that was erected in the van which contained their luggage.

The *Aide-de-Camp* made himself comfortable in the Drawing-Room on two chairs.

The Courier, the Baroness's lady's-maid, and another man whose position she was not sure of travelled in the train in reserved carriages.

Once they had started their journey from London, Toria had time to inspect the Baroness.

She was a woman of about fifty and, she thought, of Greek origin.

She had a feeling that if she was inspecting the Baroness, the Baroness was inspecting her.

She thought — and she could not quite understand why — that the Baroness was disappointed.

It was a feeling that persisted.

Finally, when late in the evening they were in the train leaving Calais, Toria sat down beside the elder woman and said:

"I do hope that you will tell me a little about your country and, of course, about the King. I am lamentably ignorant on both subjects."

There was a little pause before the Baroness replied stiffly:

"Your Royal Highness must tell me what you wish to know."

"Well, almost everything," Toria said. "I have never met anyone who had been to Klaklov, and even Lord Rosebery seems to know very little about it."

"It is a small but beautiful country."

Toria waited, and then, as the Baroness did not continue, she asked:

"And the King?"

The Baroness looked away from her.

Toria knew she was choosing her words with care.

"Did not Her Majesty Queen Victoria tell you anything about King Inged?" she enquired.

Toria shook her head.

"Her Majesty said that she had never met him since he had never been to England."

The Baroness drew in her breath before she said:

"Everyone in Klaklov is very eager that His Majesty should be married."

"Why?" Toria asked bluntly.

It was obviously a question the Baroness had not expected, and after a moment she answered:

"I expect you were told that His Majesty was married when he was very young and his wife died."

"Nobody told me that," Toria said.

"It was very sad," the Baroness replied. "They were married for only two years, and there was no child of the marriage."

"Why did the King not marry again?" Toria asked.

"I really have no idea," the Baroness answered. "We who live in the country had hoped that he would do so, and of course it is very much to our advantage that his Bride should be a relative of the great Queen Victoria."

"My Mother is English, but my Father was a Greek Prince," Toria said. "So I suppose that I am really more a Greek Princess than an English one."

The Baroness gave what was almost a cry of horror.

"No, of course not!" she said quickly. "It is absolutely essential for His Majesty to have an English Bride. That is what His Excellency asked for and what Queen Victoria has arranged."

She sounded so positive from the way she spoke that Toria thought it was a mistake to argue.

She could not help thinking, however, that her Father would be extremely annoyed.

Queen Victoria had once again brusquely swept him aside.

Then she asked herself what did it matter?

As long as she was doing what she had been asked to do and Klaklov as a country was happy, words would not make any difference to the situation.

Quite suddenly the Baroness became confidential.

"I think, Your Royal Highness," she said, "if you will forgive me for saying so, we were hoping in Klaklov that Queen Victoria would find us someone older, who would introduce a great many reforms which need to be made in our small country, and make sure her wishes were carried out."

Toria started in surprise.

"What sort of things?" she asked.

The Baroness's eyes flickered, and she looked away.

"Oh, just things that concern the country as a whole," she said. "And, of course, we need a Queen who will uphold moral standards."

Toria thought that perhaps the inhabitants of Klaklov would resent someone who was a foreigner interfering with their way of life.

Then she thought it best to say nothing.

She therefore merely continued to ask questions which she thought the Baroness answered in a very elusive manner.

"One thing is vitally important," she said finally, "and that is that I should not make any mistakes. I hope, therefore, Baroness, you will help me in every way to do what is right, and not contrary to the customs of your country."

"I will do my best, Your Royal Highness," the Baroness replied. "But it is not always easy for a woman to interfere."

Because she wanted to look out the window even though it was growing dark, Toria moved away from her.

She thought if she had to have a Lady-in-Waiting, she would rather have someone younger, certainly someone who was not disappointed in her as a person.

She wondered if there were people in Klaklov who would support her and help her to do whatever she thought was right.

Lord Rosebery had explained to her soon after her first visit to Windsor Castle that the situation was rather more difficult than it might have been.

This was because the British Consul, who had been in Klaklov for some years, had just died.

"They will appoint a replacement as soon as possible," Lord Rosebery said. "In the meantime, the staff are just carrying on as best they can, but I am afraid you will not have the support that you would have had under different circumstances."

Toria conveyed this information to her old Diplomat.

"What Lord Rosebery really means," he told Toria, "is that they are finding it difficult to persuade anyone to accept the position. After all, Klaklov is not of any importance."

He paused a moment before continuing:

"The young members of the Consular Service are ambitious and have no wish to bury themselves in the Balkans."

Toria smiled.

"I know exactly what you are saying," she said.

"They all want to go to Paris, Rome, Madrid, Berlin," the Diplomat continued. "That is where all the excitement is, not only diplomatically but socially."

"It would have been nice to think there was an Englishman to talk to if I feel lonely," Toria said almost beneath her breath.

"As soon as you are Queen," the Diplomat said, "you must write a firm letter to Lord Rosebery saying how necessary it is that the position of British Consul there should be filled."

Toria laughed.

"Do you think he will pay any attention?"

"Kings and Queens have priority," the Diplomat said. "That is the one thing no-one can deny them."

Toria laughed again.

She thought that Lord Rosebery was very nice but very authoritative.

She could not imagine his being intimidated by any letter from her however vehemently she wrote.

At the same time, she realised, when the Baroness curtsied to her and the *Aides-de-Camp* gave her the Royal Bow, that she was already on the first step of her ascent to the Throne.

"The whole question," she told herself, "is who will be sitting beside me?"

When her lady's-maid left her and she was alone in the comfortable bed in the darkened cabin, she thought of the King.

It was a story she wanted to end happily.

She told herself that the King would fall in love with her as soon as he saw her.

She would realise that he was the man who had been in her dreams.

"We will make Klaklov one of the most important countries in the Balkans," she said, "and everyone will want to visit us."

She was, however, getting rather tired of the journey by the time they reached Naples.

They then boarded the battleship that was waiting in the port.

It was a very small battleship.

Toria realised, however, as soon as she stepped aboard that the Captain and the crew were all exceedingly proud of it.

It had been decorated in her honour.

When she had been piped aboard, the Seamen all raised their caps and gave her three cheers.

That, at least, was heartening.

She enjoyed being given the Master

Cabin which she knew must have been vacated by the Captain for her.

The Mediterranean was blue and comparatively calm.

The sun was shining and Toria's spirits rose as they left Naples.

She had not been on a battleship since she was eight and had escaped with her Mother after her Father had been assassinated at Leros.

Because Princess Beatrice was English, the Navy had come to their rescue and had taken them to Marseilles.

They travelled across France by train, and on reaching England, where Princess Beatrice had been granted their Grace and Favour house at Hampton Court.

Now, because Toria had loved Leros as a child, all her memories of Greece came back.

She thought it was a good omen for the future that there was a great deal of Greek blood in the people of Klaklov.

It took them two days to pass and reach the Aegean Sea.

Toria could not help thinking that perhaps it was a good thing that her Mother was not with her.

She might have been miserable if she saw Leros again and remembered how happy she had been there.

Being a reigning Princess even on so small an island was so very different from the tiny house they had been allotted at Hampton Court.

As the Diplomat had pointed out, with only very old people to talk to, many of them had come there to die.

"Perhaps Mama will meet someone charming when she is with Lord Rosebery," Toria thought.

She had never thought of her Mother marrying again.

Yet now she knew it would be, if it occurred, a very happy solution.

"When she is well, I will insist on her coming to stay in Klaklov," she told herself. "Perhaps there will be some Greek men there who will remember Papa."

She began to feel excited at the idea of the people she could entertain.

After all, it was very different from having to count the pennies in case they could not afford to give a guest a decent meal.

She put on one of her prettiest gowns to dine with the Captain.

She was well aware from the look in his eyes, and in that of the Lieutenant Commander, that they admired her.

Each night they drew into a quiet bay so that she would not be disturbed by the noise of the engines or the movement of the ship.

On the night of the third day the Captain said to Toria:

"Tomorrow, Your Royal Highness, we shall arrive at Klaklov at noon."

"So soon," Toria said without thinking.

"We have moved slowly," the Captain explained, "because I wished Your Royal Highness to enjoy the voyage. A battleship can roll most unpleasantly if the sea is rough."

"I have enjoyed every moment!" Toria exclaimed, and knew she had pleased him.

She awoke early the next morning.

It took a little time to decide, with her lady's maid, who was a pleasant woman of about thirty, what she should wear.

Princess Beatrice had already made it easy when she had packed two suitable gowns, one thinner than the other in case the weather was warm.

The thinner dress was the prettier of the two.

When Toria put it on she looked exactly like a pale pink English rose-bud.

She knew when she went on deck that the Seamen were all looking at her with admiring eyes.

She hoped the King, when she met him, would do the same.

They moved very slowly into harbour, and she saw that there were decorations everywhere.

The Union Jack was hanging beside the Klaklovan flag.

Then, as the battleship moved slowly into the position allotted to it, she noticed that just ahead by the Quay-side there was a small cargo-boat.

Stepping off from it was a tall man.

Toria saw at a glance he was quite obviously English.

He stood out amongst the other men, who were shorter, darker, and had in a great number of cases a Greek look about them.

The Englishman was clearly giving orders about his luggage, which was being lifted ashore.

The battleship slowly moved nearer and nearer to the Quay, where there was a crowd of people waiting.

Toria could not help feeling glad that there was at least one kindred spirit in Klaklov who belonged to the same country as herself.

Impulsively she turned to the *Aide-de-*

Camp who was standing beside her and asked:

"Who is that man who has just come ashore, and who I think must be English?"

"I thought the same, Your Royal Highness," the *Aide-de-Camp* replied. "I will find out who he is."

He went away, and Toria waved to the people directly below her, who all had their faces upturned.

She saw some of them wearing elaborate uniforms.

One was obviously the Mayor, whose Chain of Office was very impressive.

She was certain that he, at any rate, would make a speech of welcome.

She only hoped she could understand it.

There was now a band playing, and as the gangplank went down, the people cheered.

Again Toria waved her hand.

Then, just as she saw the Minister of State make his way towards her to escort her ashore, the *Aide-de-Camp* came to her side.

"I have found out who the gentleman is, Your Royal Highness," he said. "He is a Mr. Terence Cliff, and he is staying in a house which belongs to another Englishman next to the British Consulate."

"Thank you," Toria said.

75

She thought it was rather childish, but she was glad there was at least one Englishman in Klaklov.

Mr. Cliff was now getting into an open carriage.

As it moved away she wondered if he was interested enough to ask who she was.

Then she told herself that although she had looked frequently at him, he had not seemed the slightest bit interested in the battleship or who was on it.

Then the Minister moved her away towards the gang-plank.

She realised as he did so that the Baroness was walking directly behind her, and behind her also there were the two *Aides-de-Camp*.

"Now I start to be a Queen," she told herself.

The cheers rang out as she walked down the gang-plank.

She had been quite right in thinking there would be a speech.

There was a long and rather solemn one.

At the same time, the Mayor welcomed her warmly to their country.

When everyone had clapped and cheered she was escorted to a very impressive carriage drawn by four white horses.

The streets were lined with people.

The horses moved very slowly so that

Toria could be seen.

She sat alone on the back seat of the carriage while the Baroness and the Minister sat opposite her.

She waved first to one side and then the other, hoping the people were genuinely pleased at her appearance.

The town itself was very pretty.

There were trees on either side of the road which were all in blossom.

The houses, which were built in a typically Balkan fashion, looked attractive, especially as most of them were decorated.

Toria found herself hoping that what she was seeing was not merely the best part of the city.

She had heard so many stories of suffering in the Balkans, of the atrocities committed by the Turks and the troubles caused by the Russians.

She was not prepared to take anything completely for granted.

Perhaps Klaklov was different, but that had yet to be proved.

They drove on, and her arms were getting a little tired of waving when finally she saw ahead the Palace.

It was on a higher level than the City and appeared to be halfway up a hill.

As the trees which framed it below and

above were in blossom, it looked exceedingly beautiful.

As she drew nearer, she saw there were elaborate wrought-iron gates touched with gold.

When they had passed through them, there were two fountains throwing their water up into the sky. It caught the sunshine and fell iridescent, like a rainbow, into the carved stone pools beneath them.

The horses climbed until they stopped where there was a long flight of steps leading up to the Palace.

They were covered with a red carpet.

There were flunkeys in elaborate uniforms on either side.

There were also soldiers who saluted when the carriages came to a standstill.

The Baroness and the Minister alighted first and then assisted Toria to the ground.

She realised she was expected to walk up the steps first.

She wondered if the King would meet her at the top of them.

She thought it rather strange that he had not come to the Quay.

She remembered that her Father had always met his guests, if they were of any importance, at the port.

She wished she had asked the Diplomat

if she could expect the King to welcome her as soon as she set foot on the soil of his country.

However, as he was not even here, she walked alone slowly up the red carpet.

She was thinking that if nothing else, the Palace was very attractive.

However, as soon as she reached the top of the steps she found there was a large number of people waiting to receive her.

She wondered which was the King.

Suddenly there was a blast of trumpets, and through an open door there appeared a man.

Toria knew without being told that this was the King.

There was no mistaking the magnificence of his uniform or the plumed hat he was wearing.

She had only a few more steps to take before she reached him.

Then, when she curtsied as her Mother had told her she must do, she heard him say, and he spoke in English:

"May I welcome Your Royal Highness to my country."

She raised her eyes and saw that he was exceedingly good-looking.

He was dark-haired and she thought his eyes were dark too.

He bent his head to kiss her hand.

Because she was shy, she had only had a quick glance at him.

His lips did not touch her hand, and almost as quickly as he had taken it he released it again.

Then, before she could say anything, he turned abruptly to walk back into the Palace.

Toria assumed that she was intended to go with him.

It took her a moment to adjust her eyes from the sunshine outside to what seemed almost like darkness inside.

Then she was aware that a man wearing an elaborate uniform was walking ahead for them to follow.

The King did not speak.

After they had gone a little way, Toria turned to look at him enquiringly.

He was staring straight ahead, and she realised his profile was clean-cut.

She wondered if she should speak, and then thought perhaps to do so would be against convention.

The man ahead of them had reached large double doors of what she realised was the Throne room.

It was already filled with a great number of people.

The women were very smartly dressed and coiffured, and the men were in uniform.

At the far end on a dais was a Throne, and beside it a lower and less impressive chair which Toria knew was for herself.

There were two steps up onto the platform.

Still without speaking, the King walked towards his throne and sat down.

Toria, after a moment's hesitation, sat on the other chair.

Immediately what seemed an unceasing flow of people climbed up on the platform to be presented.

The names were called out in a stentorian voice, and they curtsied or bowed first to the King and then to Toria.

She thought it was strange that they were not able to stop or say anything before the next names were called and other people took their place.

Some of the people looked interesting.

But a great number of them were old, and the men appeared to have important positions either at Court or in the Government.

Because she knew it was expected, Toria smiled at each one.

After a little while she could not help

being aware that the King sat stiffly in his chair.

He made no movement at all with his head.

She had the feeling, although she could not verify it, that he was simply staring straight ahead of him.

"Surely," she asked herself, "he knows all these people and might say a word or two to some of them."

Because it was a long time since she had seen or attended a Court function, she thought that perhaps what was happening was correct, that on formal occasions there was no sort of familiarity.

She was, however, quite certain it was not the way her Father had behaved when he was a Ruler.

It took nearly an hour for all the people to pass by, even though they were moving quickly.

Then they were all seated once again in the Throne room and the speeches began.

There was one from an elderly man who Toria realised was the Prime Minister.

She could understand a little of what he said.

He was followed by the Minister who had come with her from London.

He spoke partly in English, then more or

less translated his speech into his own language.

He said how gracious Queen Victoria had been in finding them a beautiful Princess to reign as Queen and how happy they were to welcome her to Klaklov.

It was all very nicely said and Toria could not help wishing she could reply in some way.

She looked at the King to see if he was appreciating the pleasant things that were being said about her.

He was still staring ahead of him.

He looked, she thought, very important and very much a King, but at the same time completely inhuman.

Then, as the people applauded what the Minister had said, she bent towards the King and said:

"If you are going to reply, do say how grateful I am for all the nice things he has just said about me."

Because people were still clapping, she spoke in quite a loud voice which he must have heard.

But to her astonishment he did not move.

He merely sat as he had before, staring in front of him.

Fearing that she had made what could

only be thought of as a social gaffe, she sat back.

Then she was aware that the Reception was at an end.

The people, having risen to clap at what the Minister had said, were not reseating themselves.

She was wondering what she should do, when the Prime Minister came to her side.

"I am sure," he said, "Your Royal Highness would like to speak to one or two of our people before they disperse."

"Yes, of course," Toria said quickly, "I would like that."

She rose to her feet.

The Prime Minister helped her down the steps on to the floor.

The people who were standing directly in front of them were introduced.

Toria shook their hands.

The General who was head of the Army spoke to her in English, while his wife could only murmur a few words in Klaklovan.

Fortunately they were simple and Toria understood.

A little hesitatingly she replied in the same language.

Both the General and the Prime Minister stared at her in surprise.

"Can you really speak Klaklovan?" they asked.

"Very little," Toria replied, "but I hope to improve. After all, a great many words are Greek."

"That is splendid," the Prime Minister said, "and I know it will endear you to our people."

He glanced at the General as he spoke, and the eyes of the two men met.

Toria was aware that there was a depth of importance behind those few simple words.

She looked back, wondering if the King was near and if he had heard what was being said.

To her astonishment, he was no longer there.

He had disappeared, and there was no sign of him.

chapter four

When the Reception was over and the guests had left, Toria was taken into the large Banqueting Hall.

There the relatives of the King and the more important Ministers were to have luncheon.

She noticed as soon as they entered the room there was still no sign of the King.

As if he knew what she was thinking, the Prime Minister said:

"I am afraid, Your Royal Highness, that His Majesty is not very well. I am only hoping it is not one of the fevers that are common in this part of the world."

"I am sorry about that," Toria replied.

She thought perhaps she had been over-critical of the King's behaviour when he had in fact been suffering.

She found herself sitting at the head of the table.

She had the Prime Minister on one side and the Minister of State who had brought her from London on the other.

The Prime Minister spoke only a little English but was fluent in Greek.

They had therefore quite an interesting conversation about the country and its people.

As soon as the meal was over, all the guests started to take their leave.

When there were finally only a few people left, the Prime Minister said:

"I thought, Your Royal Highness, if you are not too tired, you might like to drive round the city this afternoon and perhaps stop to see the Cathedral where your wedding will take place tomorrow."

"Tomorrow!" Toria exclaimed.

She had expected the wedding to be soon after she had arrived, but nobody had actually mentioned that she was to have only one day to get acclimatised to Klaklov before she married the King.

She told herself, however, that there was no point in making a fuss.

She merely said quickly:

"Of course I would enjoy a drive. I would love to see the City and the Cathedral."

She went upstairs to her bedroom.

Because she thought it was rather boring for people to see her in the same gown she had already worn in the morning, she changed.

"I am going to drive to see the City," she

told her lady's-maid, "and also the Cathedral."

To her surprise, the maid did not answer for a moment, and then she said:

"I hope Your Royal Highness will take care of yourself. There are a lot of unpleasant people about at the moment."

As she spoke in her own language it took Toria a second or two to understand what she meant.

Then she asked in surprise:

"Are you saying that I might be in danger?"

The maid looked embarrassed, as if she knew she should not have spoken so impulsively.

Toria added:

"Tell me the truth. I would much rather know what is likely to happen than be unpleasantly surprised."

There was a pause before the maid said:

"Things were bad before I came to England. I hear they've got worse since I've been away."

"What is happening? What sort of people are they?" Toria insisted.

She was quite certain that if there was any disturbance, it would be connected with the Russians.

But she wanted to know what her

maid thought of it.

The woman made a gesture with her hands.

"I don't know what is happening, Your Royal Highness," she said. "But I'll try to find out."

"Yes, do," Toria said.

She thought as she drove away with the Prime Minister, the Baroness, and the Minister of State that she might find out something from them.

"I hear," she said, "that you are having a little disturbance in Klaklov, especially in the City. Do you know who is causing it?"

The Prime Minister looked at her with an expression of consternation on his face.

"Who has been talking?" he asked sharply. "If it is one of the *Aides-de-Camp,* he will be sharply reprimanded."

"It is no-one like that," Toria answered. "I heard before I left England that you were having some trouble, but I thought everything seemed very pleasant and peaceful when I arrived."

She thought that the Prime Minister re-laxed, as if he had been afraid of her saying something different.

"There is always trouble of some sort in cities," he said casually, "and when there is a Royal Wedding, it attracts both strangers from other countries and also the worst that we possess in our own."

He glanced at the Minister of State, as he spoke, who laughed and said:

"That sums it up very clearly, Prime Minister. I can assure Her Royal Highness of a great welcome from our people to-morrow."

The open carriage was well sprung and very comfortable.

They drove along the main street and attracted very little attention.

It was certainly very different from the cheering crowds there had been in the morning.

The children were waving small Union Jacks and occasionally throwing flowers towards the Royal Carriage.

Now the women with shawls over their heads seemed to be in too much of a hurry to be interested in who was passing.

The men did not remove their caps.

They either stared or looked away in another direction.

It made Toria wonder about the scene when she had driven from the Quay to the Palace.

Had the cheering crowd been arranged by the Politicians who had been so eager to obtain a Bride from Queen Victoria?

Then she told herself she was being ridiculous.

She was merely imagining this because it was different from what she had expected.

They drove down several streets lined by well-built houses and then reached the Cathedral.

It was obviously old and Greek Orthodox, just as the Churches had been in Leros when she was there as a child.

There were the same silver lamps hanging from the ceiling in front of the Altar, and the same scent of incense.

The two Statesmen were obviously very proud of the Cathedral.

The black-bearded Priest who met them at the door showed Toria its treasures.

There were exquisitely painted icons hanging on the walls, most of them many hundreds of years old.

The Priest also explained to Toria the Wedding Ceremony.

She knew her part in it would not be difficult.

Then, when they had seen all there was to be seen, he asked Toria if he could bless her.

She knelt in front of him while he said a long Blessing in Greek which she remembered hearing when she was a child.

As they drove back towards the Palace, she thanked the Prime Minister for taking her to the Cathedral.

"It is very beautiful," she said, "and I feel sure my Wedding will be a very memorable one."

"Not only for Your Royal Highness," the Prime Minister said, "but also for the people of Klaklov."

He spoke firmly, as if he were forcing his policy on them.

Again Toria could not help wondering if the situation was worse than they wished to admit.

Queen Victoria had made it quite clear that her Wedding was to take place very soon.

Although no-one had said it to her, she had the feeling that a great number of people believed that the Wedding would free them from the menace that they were afraid to talk about.

When they arrived back at the Palace there was in Toria's honour an English Tea Party.

One of the King's relatives presided.

They had all, she was told, come to stay for the Wedding.

Even while they were having tea, several more arrived, having travelled from the farthest part of the country.

They were very pleasant to Toria.

Yet she had the feeling, just as she had with the Baroness, that they had hoped she would be older and, if possible, a replica of Queen Victoria.

"They are disappointed," she said to herself, "but there is nothing I can do about it."

Hardly any of them, naturally, could speak English, so, as she found it a struggle to speak in their language, she excused herself, saying she would like to rest before dinner.

"Of course you must rest," one of the relatives replied. "You must certainly look your best tonight, when we have planned a special dinner. We have brought all our personal presents to give to Inged before it."

"That will be exciting," Toria said.

"There are many for you too," the relatives said. "We do not think you will be disappointed in our choice."

Toria went up to her own room, where her maid was waiting.

Because she felt a little tired, she took off her gown and lay down.

She meant only to rest and think about what had happened, but she fell sound asleep.

When she awoke, it was time to dress for dinner.

She was glad she had such pretty gowns to choose from, and she wore the one which had come from the same shop as her Wedding-Dress.

It was very pale blue.

The chiffon which encircled the décolletage was scattered with tiny diamanté.

They also glittered on the sash which encircled her small waist.

She went downstairs and into the large Salon where the King's relatives had assembled.

They all exclaimed how pretty she looked and paid her compliments.

The presents — a large number of them — had been arranged on a table.

But there was again no sign of the King.

Because they suggested it, Toria began to open the gifts which had been brought for her.

The relatives had certainly been very generous.

There were brooches, necklaces, diamonds, and pearls.

One elderly relative had given her a whole set, including a tiara, of turquoises and diamonds.

It was so lovely that Toria found it difficult to express her gratitude.

"You will look beautiful in it, my dear,"
the old woman said, "as I did when I was
your age."

Toria was still trying to thank her, when
the King came in.

He looked very impressive in Evening-
Dress, wearing several decorations on his
cutaway coat.

She noticed that he walked slowly, as if
he were tired, and she thought he was
forcing the smile to his lips.

He came towards her and she said impulsively:

"I do hope Your Majesty is better."

He looked at her in surprise, as if he did
not know what she meant, and then he answered:

"I welcome Your Royal Highness to
Klaklov, and I hope you will be very
happy."

As this was the same speech he had
made to her when she arrived, Toria
looked at him in surprise.

Then, before she could reply, the relatives were all round him.

They dragged him towards the end of
the table so that he could open his presents.

As there were a number of her own still unopened, Toria thought it would seem rude if she did not busy herself with them.

Even as she did she was aware that the King was not opening his own presents and his relatives were doing it for him.

He did not seem particularly elated by what he received.

Dinner was announced, and again moving very stiffly, the King offered Toria his arm.

As they processed along the corridor towards the Banqueting Hall, Toria said:

"I was taken to see the Cathedral this afternoon. It is very beautiful, and the Prime Minister says everyone in the City is very excited about our Wedding."

For a moment there was a silence as if the King did not understand what she had said.

Then, as they reached the door of the Banqueting Hall, he said:

"Yes, yes, of course."

Then his *Aides-de-Camp* were helping him into the throne-like chair at the end of the table and Toria sat down on his right.

The dinner was excellent, and everyone seemed to be talking at once, excitedly, except the King himself.

He ate very little but drank the champagne which was followed by a number of other wines.

The Prime Minister, who was once again on Toria's other side, had a great deal to say to her.

Although she wanted to talk to the King, it was not possible to do so until the first course was finished.

As she turned towards him, she was aware an *Aide-de-Camp* was whispering in his ear.

She waited for him to be free to attend to her.

To her surprise, he turned his head sharply to say:

"You had a good journey. The ship was comfortable."

It seemed to be a statement rather than a question, and Toria replied:

"It was very exciting for me to be on a ship again. The last time was when I left Leros and I was only eight."

"Eight," the King repeated.

"My Mother and I went to England," Toria said, "because, as you know, my Father was assassinated."

"Assassinated!" the King said, and he almost shouted the word.

"Yes, assassinated," Toria answered.

"Assassinated," the King repeated. "Who is talking about assassination?"

He spoke in a loud voice that seemed to echo across the Banqueting Hall.

Quite a number of people at the table stopped talking to stare at him.

It was then that the *Aide-de-Camp* who had spoken to him before was saying something again.

In consternation, Toria turned to the Prime Minister.

"I am afraid I have upset His Majesty," she said, "by speaking of my Father's assassination."

"You could not have known," the Prime Minister said quietly, "but there was an attempt on His Majesty's life a few weeks ago."

"Nobody told me," Toria said, "and of course it must have upset him."

"It did not hurt him," the Prime Minister said. "The man was seized by the soldiers and quickly hurried away. So very few people knew what had occurred."

"Yet it must have been a shock," Toria said, "and I think, Prime Minister, you should have warned me that it was a subject I should not discuss."

The Prime Minister apologised.

Because Toria was concerned at having upset the King, she thought it best not to speak to him again.

He made no effort to speak to her.

As dinner ended, the King's most distinguished relative, who was acting as hostess, rose at the far end of the table.

The ladies followed her towards the door.

They did not, however, leave alone in the English fashion, but the gentlemen followed.

When they reached the Salon, Toria realised the King was not amongst them.

She felt it could not really be her fault that he had disappeared.

Perhaps he was again feeling ill, as he had at the Reception.

The Prime Minister was standing alone, and she went up to him.

"As His Majesty seems so ill," she said, "would it not be best to postpone the Wedding until he is better?"

"No, no, of course not," the Prime Minister said in a voice of horror. "Everything is arranged. Everything must take place exactly as it has been planned."

"But His Majesty . . ." Toria began.

"He will be perfectly all right by tomorrow," the Prime Minister said firmly. "I have already sent for his Doctors to tell them something must be done. I promise you, Princess, that you need not worry any further."

'It is all very well for him to say that,' Toria thought, and of course she worried.

When they went up to bed very shortly afterwards, she was still worried.

It was quite early, in fact only just after half-past-nine.

When the maid came hurrying to her room, surprised to see her so soon, Toria said:

"I want to write a letter to my Mother. I will ring for you when I am ready to undress."

The Maid curtsied and withdrew.

Toria sat down at the elegant French *Secrétaire* which stood in the corner of her bedroom.

She realised she had a *Boudoir* next door, and beyond that lay the King's apartments.

She thought, however, she would rather stay in her bedroom.

She sat down and pulled a piece of embossed writing-paper onto the blotter.

She thought she heard a noise through the open window which sounded like the report of a gun.

She rose and looked out.

It was impossible to see very much through the blossom of the trees.

'I must have imagined it,' she thought, and sat down again to write her letter.

She tried to describe to her Mother what had happened since her arrival.

It made her realise how little she could tell her about the man she was to marry.

'It is ridiculous that I am not able to talk to him,' she thought, and put down her pen.

'I want to see him alone before we are actually married,' she decided.

She had the feeling that in some way everyone in the Palace had been keeping them apart.

Moreover, if the King were really ill, whatever the Prime Minister might say, it was absurd that they should be married tomorrow.

She rose to her feet and walked towards the door.

She looked out into the wide corridor and realised that since she had come upstairs, the candles had burnt out.

They were in sconces which were all of gold embossed with the King's insignia.

She glanced towards the King's bedroom which was past her own and at the end of the corridor.

As she did so, she saw a man coming out of it who looked, she thought, like a valet.

Making up her mind, she walked towards him.

As she reached him, she said slowly in Klaklovan:

"Will you please ask His Majesty if I could see him for a few minutes? Or, if he is too ill, I would like to talk to his Doctor."

The servant stared at her.

As he understood what she said, he bowed and went back through the door from which he had just come.

Toria did not follow him, she just waited in the passage.

If the King thought it was a strange request, she had at least done her best to help him if he was ill.

At least she had tried to get to know him a little better before the moment that she became his wife.

More quickly than she expected, the servant returned.

"Will Your Royal Highness go in," he said.

He opened the door as he spoke, and Toria walked through it.

She found herself in a small hall, with two doors opening out of it, which was lit by a chandelier.

As she hesitated, she heard the door that led into the corridor close behind her and knew the servant had left.

Then the door in front of her opened, and

to her surprise a young woman stood there.

She was rather attractive with dark hair.

She was wearing a strange garment which looked more like a negligee than an evening-gown.

She looked at Toria and then said in Greek:

"I am Arina, and I hear you want to see the King."

There was something pert in the way she spoke with a twist of her red lips.

"I have come to see His Majesty," Toria said, "as I understand he is ill."

The woman facing her laughed.

"He is all right now," she said. "Come and see for yourself."

She opened the door wide through which she had come and Toria moved forward.

She found herself in a very large room, in the centre of which was a huge, canopied bed.

Lying on it, wearing apparently nothing but a purple satin robe, was the King.

He was lying back against a mountain of pillows, and beside him lay a girl, also dark-haired, who appeared to be asleep.

She was semi-naked with one breast bare.

Her nightgown, or whatever it was she was wearing, was pulled up to reveal her naked legs.

Because Toria could not believe what she was seeing, she could only stare at the King and the sleeping girl.

The King looked at her first in surprise, then he exclaimed:

"So you have come to join us. That is good. Now we can be more cheerful. I told you, Arina, she was very pretty. Give her something to make her prettier still."

He spoke in a bright, cheerful voice which was very different from the way he had spoken to Toria before.

He was smiling.

His eyes, although they were so dark that the pupils seemed to be dilated, were shining.

His hair was tousled, and as he moved she could see his bare chest.

"Inged is right," Arina said. "Now come and choose what you are going to have. If you are a complete novice, you had better begin with cocaine."

For a moment Toria did not recognise the word in Greek.

Then as she saw, on a gold-carved table against the wall with a marble top, a number of packages, she understood that she was being offered drugs.

It was something she had never dreamt of happening in her life.

Arina busied herself with opening a small packet she had taken from a china plate which contained several more.

Toria gave a little murmur of horror.

Then, before she could speak or realize what was happening, she felt the King's arm go round her and pull her close to him.

He had got off the bed without her being aware of it.

Now, because he was tall and she was very much smaller, she felt her cheek touch the silk of his robe and she was aware of the closeness and the nakedness of him.

"Now we will enjoy ourselves," the King said in a thick voice, "and here we do not have to worry about those croaking, gloomy Politicians."

He pulled her closer as he spoke.

Then she was aware of his hand pushing aside the chiffon which encircled her décolletage and his fingers feeling for her breasts.

She gave a little scream and struggled against the King.

Inadvertently as she did so she stamped, wearing her hard-soled slipper, on his bare foot.

He gave an exclamation of pain, and his

hold on her loosened.

In that moment she was free.

She ran across the room, pulled open the door, crossed the small hall, and let herself out into the corridor.

Then, without looking back, she ran more swiftly than she had ever run before to her own room.

Only when she reached it and had slammed the door and locked it did she manage to draw in her breath.

With a murmur of sheer horror she flung herself down on the bed.

It seemed quite a long time before Toria forced herself to think clearly.

As she went back in her mind over what had occurred, she felt it could not really be true.

The Prime Minister and all the responsible members of the Government must have been aware that the King was a drug-addict.

Yet they had dared to come to England to ask Queen Victoria to give him a Bride who would be a protection for their country.

She could understand now why it had been difficult to find out anything about the King.

She imagined that it had been particularly to the advantage of the Statesmen that the British Consul, who might have been aware of the situation at the Palace, had died.

It was something that obviously had to be kept as secret as possible from the outside world.

Toria knew very little about drugs.

Yet she guessed that his attendants had somehow managed to keep the King from taking any before he met her on her arrival, and before he had to appear at dinner.

Now there was an explanation for his lethargy, for his apparent difficulty in understanding anything that was being said!

Without the support of the drug he could only stare sightless in front of him, oblivious to all around him.

It was only the drug which could exhilarate him, as he was at this moment.

She supposed that eventually, when the King and Arina had taken as much as the other girl who lay lifeless on the bed, they would all sink into an oblivion until the morning came.

Her mind stopped as she remembered that tomorrow was the Wedding-Day.

She was to be married to a man who had just touched her, a man for whom she had a revulsion as strong as if he were a poisonous reptile.

She could still feel the strength of his arm round her body and his fingers fumbling for her breast.

It made her feel unclean, and she wanted to wash herself.

At the same time, she knew it would be impossible to forget the horror of what had just happened.

She rose from the bed.

The appalling problem was what could she do?

She walked to the window, desperately trying to think clearly, still feeling so shocked by what she had experienced that all she wanted to do was to run and to go on running.

Then she realised she had been enticed into a trap from which she could not escape.

She had to admit it was a clever trap of the Statesmen of Klaklov.

They wanted the security that would be theirs through her being a relative of the most powerful Monarch in the world.

At the same time, as a woman she would be married to a man whom she knew she would despise, a man who would drag her down to the depths of depravity to which he had sunk.

She stood at the window, feeling as if she were gasping for air.

She felt the prison walls were closing in irrevocably, and after tomorrow there would be no escape ever.

It was then she knew that she had to get away — at once.

Whatever the consequences, however angry everyone might be, anything would be better than being married to the man she had just left.

She felt as if she were still looking at the girl lying half-naked on the bed.

She had slipped into unconsciousness because of the drugs she had taken.

She could understand now the darkness of the King's eyes with their dilated pupils, and the darkness in Arina's.

The lilt in their voices, the excitement of their bodies, was all part of the drug they had taken and was unnatural, just as everything they did during the night would be unnatural and perverted.

"I have to get away," Toria murmured beneath her breath.

She knew it would be terribly difficult, if not impossible.

Then she heard the old Diplomat at Hampton Court Palace saying:

"You must have courage. Courage to follow your heart and your soul."

It was almost as if it were a message from God and an answer to prayer.

She looked round her room and then went to the wardrobe.

All the beautiful gowns she and her Mother had bought in Bond Street were hanging there.

She chose one of the plainest.

It was a pretty gown in a deep blue which Princess Beatrice had thought she might need for travelling.

There was a short jacket to go with it.

Toria changed very quickly.

Now she tried to think of what she would need to take with her.

The most important thing was money.

She would have to pay her fare back to England.

As it was such a long distance, it would undoubtedly be expensive.

Unfortunately, she had very little money with her.

It had not seemed necessary, and she wanted to leave her Mother everything she could.

Then she remembered the jewellery that she had been given only that afternoon, also the presents she had received when she was in England.

Besides paying for her trousseau, Queen Victoria had sent her a diamond brooch in the shape of a Crescent.

It had been, Toria thought somewhat cynically, not so much a present for her as for the people of Klaklov.

There was a very pretty bracelet which had been a present from Lord Rosebery.

There was also a gift which, Toria thought, would impress the Statesmen of Klaklov.

It was an enamel box ornamented with a diamond crown which had been delivered from the Prime Minister, the Marquess of Salisbury.

She collected these last three pieces and put them into her handbag.

Then she saw that the gifts which she had received downstairs had been brought up while they were at dinner and laid on top of the chest-of-drawers.

For a moment she hesitated.

Then she knew she wanted to take nothing from the people of Klaklov, especially from the relatives of the King.

They would doubtless be horrified at her behaviour when they learnt she had gone.

At the same time, they would be able to work out why.

"They must have known what he was

like. Of course they knew what he was like," she said beneath her breath.

Among the clothes she had brought from London there was a blue silk shawl.

It had been given her by the Dressmaker from whom they had bought the most expensive gowns.

"It is something you will find useful, Your Royal Highness, to put over your shoulders in the evening," she said. "It is always the same in those foreign countries. It is hot in the daytime, then the winds come down from the mountains and one shivers at dinner-time."

Toria had laughed but thanked her warmly.

Now she laid the shawl on the bed and put on it some things she would need before she reached home.

A nightgown, some silk underclothes, and because it was so light, a little chiffon gown to be worn either in the afternoon or the evening.

Then she tied the ends of the scarf together.

The bundle did not look too large or conspicuous.

The first and main problem was how she could get out of the Palace.

She looked again in the wardrobe.

Her Mother had bought for her as an evening-wrap a long cape of dark blue velvet.

Because it was meant for the summer, it was not trimmed with fur.

When Toria put it on over the gown she was wearing, she thought it was very concealing.

There was a scarf in one of her drawers which was made of chiffon.

She covered her head with it.

She thought if she carried her bundle under the cape and kept in the shadows, it was possible that no-one would notice her.

Since, of course, she did not know her way around the Palace, there was a danger of being noticed wandering about.

However, she knew where the grand staircase was, up which she had come to bed.

She was quite certain there must be other staircases leading down to the ground-floor on which there would be no attendant footmen.

She picked up her bundle and walked to the door.

She unlocked it and transferred the key to the lock outside.

She thought that locking it would delay people from forcing their way into the room, as they would assume she was asleep.

It was then she remembered the communicating-door into the *Boudoir*.

She went back to lock that.

Then, with her heart beating so violently that she thought anyone passing would hear it, she locked her bedroom door and removed the key.

She started to creep down the passage past the King's bedroom.

He was without doubt laughing at her for not joining him.

He would be sweeping away his inhibitions as he took more and more of the drugs that were waiting for him on the gold-carved table.

Toria hurried on, thankful that there was no sign of anyone in the corridor.

She found what she was seeking.

A small staircase very sparingly lit, which meant that it was unimportant, led down to the ground-floor.

She stepped down it and found, as she was expecting, that she was at the far end of the Palace.

There was no-one to be seen.

It did not take her long to find a door which opened onto the garden.

It was bolted, but the key was in the lock.

In only a few seconds she was able to

step out into the coolness of the night air.

Now she knew she had only to escape from the garden of the Palace to be in the streets of the City itself.

The question was where she should go then.

Suddenly, as if it were in answer to her question, or perhaps once again she was praying for help, she thought of the Englishman, the man she had seen disembarking on the Quay as the battleship had moved in to where those who had come to receive her were waiting.

She remembered his name was Terence Cliff.

She remembered, too, that the *Aide-de-Camp* had told her that he was staying in a house beside the British Consulate.

'I will appeal to him to help me,' Toria thought.

She had met members of the Consulate at the Reception and knew that they would be no help whatsoever.

They consisted only of an elderly man who was obviously not very well bred, and two young Englishmen who were little more than clerks.

She was quite certain that they would not do anything which might offend Queen Victoria.

They might actually force her to return to the Palace, just as any of the Statesmen and Politicians of Klaklov would do.

'The Englishman is my only hope,' Toria told herself as she moved across the garden.

Then she realised there would be sentries on all the gates, and she had to somehow pass them.

She soon reached one of the gates and stood in the shelter of some bushes nearby.

There were two sentries on the gate, and they were talking to each other.

The gate was a large one, and because it was still early in the evening, it was open, not half-closed, as she was sure it would have been later.

She hesitated.

She bravely walked forward, hoping they would think she had been a visitor to the Palace. But then she stopped.

Suddenly several roughly-dressed men came up to talk to them.

They were obviously friends.

When the newcomers started to talk in what Toria thought was a somewhat aggressive manner, the two sentries listened attentively.

It was difficult to understand what they were saying.

They spoke very quickly and their voices were uncultured.

Their language sounded very different from that spoken by the Prime Minister or the Minister of State.

Toria had the impression that the new-comers were asking the sentries to do something for them.

Whatever it was was unimportant.

What mattered was that they were discussing it very intently and arguing quite heatedly.

Moreover, she realised that on one side the gate-way was quite dark.

The light from the lantern shone on the other side, where the sentries and the men talking to them were all standing together in a bunch.

Holding her breath and praying that she would not be seen, she moved from the bushes.

Then the men's voices rose and they suddenly laughed loudly, as if at some joke.

As the noise vibrated in the air, she slipped through the gate and into the street outside.

She did not do anything so foolish as to run, but she walked very swiftly away.

For the moment, she was not thinking where she was going, only grateful to have escaped from her prison.

When she knew she was out of sight of the sentries, who had obviously not seen her, she tried to think clearly.

The Prime Minister had pointed out the British Consulate to her on their way to the Cathedral, which was very fortunate.

She thought she could remember where it was.

Once she saw it again, it would be impossible to be mistaken about the formal, upright building with the Union Jack on a flagpole outside it.

The streets were almost deserted, and she walked quickly.

She was afraid she might attract the attention of some man or, worse still, pickpockets or thieves.

No-one, however, seemed to give her a second glance.

She heard voices sounding somewhat rowdy in the darkness.

They came from the equivalent of what in England would be an Inn or a Bar where liquor could be bought and drunk.

She must have walked for twenty minutes before she found herself in the Square through which she had driven in the morning and where the Prime Minister had pointed out the British Consulate.

It was there exactly as she remembered.

There were only a few lights in the top windows, and the flagpole was bereft for the night of the Union Jack.

Then she stopped and took her bearings.

There was a house on one side of it which looked impressive and was obviously what in England would have been described as "a Gentleman's Residence."

She looked on the other side.

To her great relief, there was no choice.

On the other side of the Consulate there was a long, low building which might have been a gymnasium or a school.

Toria looked back again at the private house.

This she knew was a very crucial moment.

If she were not offered help, it might be very difficult for her to get away once it was discovered she was missing.

As she walked she had been thinking.

It was almost as if her Guardian Angel were helping her.

She knew exactly the story she must tell to make the Englishman be sympathetic and willing to assist her to leave Klaklov, even if it meant she could only, at first, get as far as Greece.

"I will go to Leros," she reasoned. "I am sure I can find someone there who will help me for Papa's sake."

There was, however, one thing of which she was absolutely certain.

It was imperative that no-one should suspect for a moment that she was the Princess who had come to Klaklov to marry the King.

If anyone did, she would find herself back in the Palace and never have the chance to escape again.

"Help me, Papa, help me," she said as she looked ahead of her at the front-door.

It was almost as if he were beside her.

She heard her Father saying the same words the Diplomat had said to her:

"Have courage, and follow your heart and your soul."

chapter five

The Duke of Cannuncliff sat contemplating three pictures with a smile of satisfaction.

He thought he should be very grateful to his cousin. He had been staying in Venice when he received a letter from his cousin, saying:

> *My dear Terence,*
>
> *You will be surprised to read my address, but I have just taken a house here for six months while I write about this strange little country.*
>
> *Soon after I arrived, a man offered me a very fine Guardi, and because he asked only 500 pounds, I bought it for you.*
>
> *He then intimated that he had a number of other pictures for sale, and I surmised, without probing too deeply, that there was something suspicious about where they came from.*
>
> *In fact, I have the idea, although I may be quite wrong, that he has something to do with the Palace. Anyway, the picture is undoubtedly authentic, and I know it will delight you.*

I suggest you come here as soon as possible and see what other pickings there may be in this rather strange place.

My house is at your disposal and is quite comfortable.

I shall certainly be delighted to see you.

Yours,
Robert

The Duke had read the letter carefully, and thought it was extraordinary that his cousin should have found a Guardi in Klaklov, and going so cheap.

He knew he could trust his cousin's judgement, and his taste was exceptionally good.

He therefore decided without any further delay to go to Klaklov immediately.

His Cousin Robert knew, as did most of his relatives, that he had set himself a task.

It was to restore the Picture Gallery of Cannun to its original splendour.

Unfortunately the two previous Dukes had not been at all interested in Art.

They had spent their money on horses and, if the gossips were to be believed, on beautiful and expensive women.

The collection of pictures in the Gallery had therefore deteriorated.

The present 6th Duke, who had never

expected to inherit, being only the younger son, had always been obsessed with Art.

He had spent what little money he had as an unimportant member of the family visiting all the Art Galleries of Europe.

When he came into the title, the huge Estates, and a very considerable fortune, his first thought was —

"Now I can buy the pictures I need."

He had come to Venice for that very reason.

He had first managed to purchase a very fine Caravaggio, when he received his Cousin Robert's letter.

Robert Cliff, who was a good deal older than the Duke, had decided that he would write a book on the Balkans.

He was taking his time about it.

He had stayed in many different Balkan countries where, because of his Ducal connection and his personal charm, he was invariably invited to the Palace.

That he had taken a house in Klaklov told the Duke that he was settling down to put together the material he had collected.

He looked forward to reading the book when it was completed.

The Duke had his yacht with him in Venice.

As he sailed down the coast of Albania, he thought it would be a mistake, if he wished to get the pictures Robert had written about cheaply, to appear in what he was sure was a very small harbour at Klaklov in "*The Siren of the Sea.*"

This was the name of his yacht, a new acquisition of which he was very proud.

She was undoubtedly spectacular.

The Duke knew that after one glance at her, the price for the pictures would double or treble.

This was one of the reasons he usually travelled not as the Duke of Cannuncliff, but as Terence Cliff.

There were a large number of Cliffs in existence.

No one in the small countries of the Balkans would be likely to query that he was anything but what he professed to be.

He therefore decided, as "*The Siren of the Sea*" rounded the south of Greece and sailed up the Aegean Sea, he would stop at a small Port in Eastern Macedonia.

His maps told him there were some rivers ending in small ports which flowed into the sea just before one reached Klaklov.

This was not the first time since he had inherited that he had travelled with his yacht incognito.

The Captain and every Seaman aboard knew that they faced dismissal if they revealed to anyone his true identity.

He therefore instructed his Captain where to dock.

There was, as he had expected, a small port at the mouth of the river Struma.

It flowed from the North of Macedonia into the sea a short distance from the Port of Klaklov.

From there the Duke managed to find a cargo-boat that was sailing to Klaklov.

He spent a somewhat uncomfortable night aboard her.

He was carried safely into the Port early in the morning.

There was no difficulty in finding his cousin's house.

However, he discovered on arrival that Robert Cliff had left a note for him in which he had written:

I have no idea when you may arrive, and I have had an invitation from the King of Siberia to stay for some unusual festivity which would certainly add interest to my book.

You must therefore forgive me if I am an "absent host." Make yourself comfortable, and I promise you I shall be back in a week or ten days.

The couple who look after me are effi-

cient and cook well. They speak quite a lot of Greek, so I am sure you will manage to get everything you require.

I am hoping, perhaps optimistically, that I shall be back before you arrive.

Yours,
Robert

The Duke had managed to make the man and woman understand exactly what he required.

They helped him to get in touch with the man who had sold his cousin the Guardi.

It was certainly a very fine example of the Master's work.

He knew it was exceedingly cheap at the price Robert had paid for it.

As his cousin had said, there was obviously something suspect about these pictures being for sale.

To begin with, the vendor would speak only in a whisper in his scruffy shop.

He informed the Duke that he would show him some pictures immediately, but he would bring them to the Duke's house.

He warned him not to tell anyone in Klaklov why he was there.

He must not even say that he was interested in pictures.

Having said all this in a *sotto voce* garlic-smelling whisper, he hurried the Duke out of his shop.

He promised to come to his house next to the British Consulate as soon as possible.

The Duke thought the whole transaction was indeed suspiciously furtive.

He walked round the City and looked in at the Cathedral.

He was informed that a Royal Wedding was to take place there the next day.

He then returned to his cousin's house.

The couple had prepared him an edible meal.

With it he drank some excellent white wine which his cousin had left for him.

He was wondering if the pictures he hoped for were just a myth, when the man arrived with two.

They were both exceptionally fine examples of their artist's work.

One was *"The Madonna and Child"* by Morales, the other *"Apollo and Daphne"* by N. Poussin.

Neither picture was framed.

The way the man who brought them spoke of them made the Duke suspect they had been stolen.

At the same time, he thought it impossible for anyone to get away with stealing anything so valuable.

In so small a country the thief would come under suspicion almost as soon as the theft was discovered.

Again the prices asked were ridiculously low.

In fact, both pictures were such a bargain that the Duke felt it was really too embarrassing to haggle over the price.

He was sure, however, that that was what the Vendor would expect.

He was only surprised when the small reduction he suggested was accepted immediately.

Because the country was small, no vendor would have risked accepting and presenting a cheque.

The Duke had therefore brought a large amount of ready money with him.

He was able to pay for the transaction in cash.

He was aware that the man who had brought him the pictures was delighted with the deal.

"Are there any more where these came from?" the Duke asked.

"Yes, yes!" was the answer. "Many pictures, but difficult obtain more than one or two at a time."

The Duke raised his eye-brows, but said

nothing and the man went on:

"I try. I try and bring you, Sir, one day after to-morrow, perhaps more by end of week."

He was obviously working out something complicated in his mind.

The Duke waited, wondering why the owner of the pictures was parting with them at such exceptionally ridiculous prices.

Finally he said:

"I am very interested in acquiring more, but I am afraid I cannot stay long in Klaklov. So the sooner you bring them to me, the better."

"I try — I certainly try, Sir!" the man exclaimed.

Then, as if he wished to get on with the transaction immediately, he left.

Watching him from the window, the Duke saw him almost running down the street.

He obviously did not want to waste any time in reaching his goal.

'There is something very strange going on here,' the Duke thought.

He then told himself it was none of his business.

He had bought the pictures in good faith. If the owner of them was ready to sacrifice them at about a tenth of what they were worth, that was his affair.

He knew only that they would adorn the Picture Gallery at Cannun like jewels.

He must find frames worthy of them.

The two servants provided him with a pleasant dinner.

When it was finished, they asked him if there was anything else he required for the night.

The Duke realised they now thought themselves off-duty, and he merely replied:

"I have everything, thank you. Call me at eight o'clock, and I would like breakfast at half-past."

The man bowed to show he understood.

The Duke spread out the three pictures and sat down to contemplate them.

Toria raised the knocker on the door in front of her.

Then she let it fall so gently that it hardly made a sound.

Because she was ashamed of her own fears, she picked it up again.

This time it made a loud "rat-tat."

There was only silence, and she thought despairingly that perhaps the Englishman had gone out.

She might have to wait until he returned.

Then, to her relief, she heard footsteps.

A moment later the door opened and a woman stood there.

In her somewhat halting Klaklovan, Toria said:

"Please, I want to speak to Mr. Terence Cliff."

The woman was staring at her.

She had the feeling that she might say he was not "At home" and close the door.

Instead, the woman beckoned her in.

With a little gasp of relief Toria entered the house.

The woman shut the door.

Then, as if she were surprised to find Toria waiting beside her, she pointed with her hand towards the top of the stairs.

"Up there!" she said abruptly.

Toria needed no further invitation.

She walked quickly up the stairs.

There was a door at the top of them which she thought must be the entrance to the Sitting-Room.

She remembered that in Leros most of the larger houses had their Sitting-Rooms or Drawing-Rooms on the First Floor.

Tentatively she opened the door ahead of her.

One glance told her that, as she had expected, it was the Sitting-Room.

It had three windows on the opposite

131

side of the door.

Then she saw, and she had not noticed him immediately because he was sitting down, the man she was seeking.

He had his back to her.

He was looking at some pictures which were arranged on three chairs facing him.

She did not speak.

After a moment, as if the silence surprised him, the Duke turned his head.

He had expected to see either the man-servant or the woman.

Instead, standing in the doorway was one of the prettiest young women he had ever seen.

Her head was covered with a blue chiffon veil.

She wore a dark cloak which covered her body from neck to feet.

Slowly he rose to his feet.

As he did so, Toria found her voice.

She moved forward, saying rather quickly because she was nervous:

"I . . . I have come to see you because . . . I need your help. Please . . . help me! I know you are English, as I am, and there is no one else to whom I can turn at this moment."

"You need help?" the Duke asked. "Then, of course, as you must be aware, the British Consulate is next door."

"Y-yes . . . I know," Toria replied, "but I cannot go to them . . . and that is why I have . . . come to . . . you."

She spoke in such an agitated fashion that the Duke said in a soothing voice:

"Now, suppose you sit down and tell me what your trouble is."

He indicated, as he spoke, a sofa placed near the fireplace.

Although it was hot in the daytime, there was often a cold wind at night.

It came from the not so far distant mountains.

The man-servant, quite unnecessarily, the Duke thought, had lit a small fire just before dinner.

Toria sat down on the sofa.

The Duke stood with his back to the fireplace.

"Now, tell me what this is all about," he invited Toria.

He was sure, as he spoke, that this would be a question of money.

Yet the woman calling on him certainly did not look poor.

She undid the clasp at the neck of her cloak.

The Duke with his experienced eye realised that her gown was a very expensive one.

"I . . . I am sorry to trouble you," Toria

133

began, "but . . . I know of no . . . one else in . . . the City who is . . . English . . . and I have . . . to leave this country . . . immediately!"

"Are you afraid to tell me why?" the Duke enquired.

Toria hesitated.

She had thought her story out carefully, but knew she had to convince Mr. Cliff that it was genuine.

Because she felt shy, she looked away from him as she said:

"I . . . I arrived here only . . . to-day . . . but I find the . . . situation for which . . . I had been . . . engaged is . . . intolerable! That is why I must . . . return to England."

The Duke unexpectedly moved from standing in front of the fireplace to sit down on a chair next to the sofa.

He was facing Toria directly. She had the feeling he was looking at her penetratingly, as if to make certain she was telling him the truth.

"You had an engagement to come here," he said quietly. "What sort of engagement?"

"I had been asked when I was in London to look after the children of . . . someone . . . important in Klaklov . . . and teach them English."

"In other words, you came here as a

134

Governess," the Duke said as if he were trying to get it clear in his mind.

"Th-that is . . . right," Toria agreed, "but when I arrived . . . I found that the . . . Mother of the . . . children had left her husband and taken the . . . children with her."

"You say she has left her husband," the Duke remarked. "Do you mean — for good?"

"I . . . I do not know . . . exactly," Toria said. "I was only told she had left . . . then the man . . . in-insulted me."

She stumbled over the word, and after a moment the Duke said in surprise:

"You mean — he made advances to you although he had never seen you before?"

"Yes . . . that is . . . right," Toria agreed.

She was thinking of King Inged as she spoke and how he had pushed his hand down the front of her gown.

The colour flared in her cheeks.

"I am not surprised you are upset," the Duke said sharply. "What is the man's name?"

Toria had anticipated this question, and she replied quickly:

"It is best for you not to know. He is very important and, I am sure, dangerous. He may try to stop me from leaving the country . . . because he has paid my fare here. That

135

is why I must . . . get away . . . quickly."

She paused.

Then she said in a voice the Duke could hardly hear:

"I . . . I am afraid . . . I have no . . . money!"

This is what the Duke had expected.

For a moment it flashed through his mind that it was a con-trick, and a rather clever one.

Then almost as if she could read his thoughts, Toria said:

"I mean I have . . . no ready money . . . at the . . . same time, I have . . . some jewellery which I can . . . give you . . . or perhaps you could . . . sell for me."

She took from her hand-bag the diamond crescent brooch which Queen Victoria had given her.

She held it out to the Duke.

"I think . . . this is . . . worth quite a . . . lot of money," she said. "Enough . . . at any rate . . . to get me . . . home."

"And where is your home when you are in England?" the Duke asked.

This was again a question Toria had anticipated, and she replied without a pause:

"It is in the Country . . . not far from Windsor."

"And that is where you wish to return?"

"Yes, yes . . . of course."

As she spoke, Toria could not help thinking that once she reached England, it was the last place she would go.

She was quite certain if she did and went to Hampton Court Palace, Queen Victoria, Lord Rosebery, and the Prime Minister would all insist on her returning immediately to Klaklov to marry the King.

She knew they would not be concerned with his private life or how she dealt with it.

This was a political marriage and she must reign as Queen, whatever the King was like.

"I shall have to hide somewhere," she told herself, "but first I must get away from here."

She was aware that the Duke was watching her face.

Because she suddenly felt frantic, she begged:

"Please, help me . . . there is no one else I can ask . . . and I . . . have to leave . . . I have to!"

Now there was a note of panic in her voice.

The Duke could see the terror in her eyes.

He knew no actress, however talented, could speak in such a way unless what she was saying was genuine.

"Of course I will help you," he said after a moment. "At the same time, you are quite sure you are wise in rushing away without giving the situation a trial?"

"I . . . cannot do that! It is . . . impossible!" Toria said. "As I have told you . . . the children I came to teach are . . . not here."

"You do not think it would be a good idea if I talked to your employer," the Duke suggested, "and told him he must behave himself?"

Toria gave a cry of horror.

"No . . . no, of course not! He would not . . . listen to you and would . . . force me . . . to stay! I would . . . rather . . . die . . . he is horrible . . . bestial!"

Now the Duke could see that her fingers were trembling.

He rose to his feet.

"I can see you have had a shock," he said. "I am going to pour you a glass of wine, then we will decide what is the best thing we can do for you."

He went to a table that was set in a corner of the room, on which the man-servant had placed a tray containing what was left of the bottle of wine he had drunk at dinner.

Having poured out a glass, the Duke put it beside her.

Her hands were still trembling as she accepted it.

Because she knew he was being kind, she took a small sip.

"Drink a little more," the Duke said. "It will not hurt you."

She obeyed him because it was easier to do so than argue.

Then he sat down again and said:

"Now we must make plans. You want to go to England and I will try and find out what ships are likely to be calling at this small Port. At the same time, you must be aware that you should not travel alone."

"I shall be all right," Toria said.

Looking at her, the Duke thought of a number of reasons why this was most unlikely.

Although she was pale, and he knew it was from agitation, she was the most beautiful person he had seen for a long time.

And although she spoke perfect English and said that she was English, there was something different about her from any English girl he had ever met.

Because he was silent, Toria said a little nervously:

"If I cannot get to England . . . or it is

too expensive . . . I think I could go to some friends in Greece."

"I was just thinking that perhaps you had an affinity with Olympus," the Duke said with a smile.

"I wish that were true," Toria said. "Then I could hide there . . . and no-one would find me."

"So you think you have to hide!" the Duke remarked. "Why should this man be so frightening? Surely, having behaved in such a disgraceful way, he will realise that you have no wish to stay in his house and are free to leave without his permission?"

"He paid my fare . . . and there were some expenses in London," Toria said a little lamely, "and I think he would be very angry that I was leaving after there having been so much trouble about my coming here."

It sounded even to her own ears rather unconvincing, but the Duke said:

"Then I can only hope that we will find a decent ship that will carry you at least as far as Athens. But it may take time."

"Time?" Toria exclaimed. "But I cannot stay in Klaklov! I must leave at once!"

"I am afraid that will be impossible," the Duke said, "but I will, of course, make enquiries."

"I . . . I wish to leave to-night," Toria insisted.

The Duke smiled and made a gesture with his hands.

"That really is impossible — unless you can fly like a bird!"

Toria was silent.

The Duke picked up the diamond crescent which he had taken from her and put it on the arm of the sofa.

"Put this away in your hand-bag," he said. "When we find some way of conveying you to England, I will give you the money for your fare. You can pay me back when you can afford to do so."

"Oh, thank you . . . thank you!" Toria exclaimed. "You are so very, very kind, as I knew you would be!"

"How could you know that I would be?" the Duke asked. "And how did you find me here in the first place?"

"I saw you when I was driving through the City," Toria said. "I was sure you were English and I asked your name."

The Duke seemed to accept this, but she hoped he would not in any way connect her with the battleship that had come into the Port at the same time as he was disembarking.

Because she felt nervous she picked up

the glass she had put down on a small table beside the sofa and drank a little more of the wine.

As she did so, there was the sudden sound of a gun being fired.

The Duke raised his head and walked to the open window.

"That sounded like a gun-shot!" he said.

"It did sound like it!" Toria agreed.

When there were no more shots, the Duke shut the window.

"It is getting late, and I therefore suggest you stay the night here. First thing in the morning I will go down to the Quay and find out if there is any available ship, and see what it is like."

"I . . . I can . . . stay here?" Toria said almost beneath her breath.

"That is what I said," the Duke answered. "If you keep out of sight, I imagine no-one will be particularly interested in my having a guest staying with me."

"Thank you! Thank you very much indeed!" Toria said. "I was afraid of walking about late at night in the streets."

"Of course you were," the Duke agreed, "and it is something you should never do! Now — let us find you a bedroom."

Toria took the cloak from her shoulders and put it over her arm.

Carrying a shawl which contained everything she possessed, she followed the Duke from the room.

The bedrooms were beyond the Sitting-Room, and there were two of them; the guest-room which he was occupying himself, and his Cousin's room.

He took Toria into that one and saw it was well-furnished.

He was sure the bed-linen had already been changed.

"Sleep well," he said, "and I am sure that tomorrow we shall find a solution to your problem."

"I shall be thanking God that I saw you when I did, and knew that when I was in trouble you would help me," Toria said in a low voice. "And once I have got away, there will be no need for me to trouble you again."

"Let us take one fence at a time," the Duke said, "and the most difficult one is to find the right sort of ship."

He had brought one of the lighted candles from the Sitting-Room, and now he put it down on the dressing-table.

"Is there anything I can get you?" he asked.

"No, no," Toria answered. "I have everything I need, and thank you . . . thank you from the bottom of my heart!"

The Duke smiled, then went out and shut the door behind him.

When she was sure he had gone, Toria put her hands together and said a prayer that came from the depths of her heart.

She had escaped — so far she had escaped — and somehow, by some miracle, Mr. Cliff would get her out of the country.

Toria was fast asleep when she was awoken by a loud knocking on the door.

For a moment she thought she was at home and it was her Mother who wanted her.

Then, as she sat up in bed, the door opened and the Duke said:

"Get up quickly and dress! We have to leave immediately!"

"Im-immediately?" Toria repeated.

"There is trouble in the City," the Duke explained, "and the sooner we are out of the country, the better!"

"What is happening?" Toria asked.

But already he had gone, and because she knew from the way he had spoken that she really had to hurry, she jumped out of bed.

It did not take long to dress, and she had only her nightgown to pack.

When she came out of the room the door on the other side of the corridor was open, and she thought that the Duke would be downstairs.

She was correct in that assumption.

She could hear his voice in the hall as he talked to the man-servant, who was gesticulating with his hands, his voice rising in a high crescendo as he spoke.

As Toria came down the stairs, the Duke said:

"Ah, here you are! Eat something as quickly as you can, then we must leave!"

There was coffee and some rolls and butter on the table in what was obviously the Dining-Room.

Toria drank a little of the coffee, and as the Duke joined her, she asked:

"Tell me — what is happening?"

"Apparently a great number of people in the City are objecting to the wedding which is to take place to-day."

"Wedding?" Toria murmured.

"They do not want an English Queen, and have for some time been trying to rid themselves of their King," the Duke explained. "Anyway, it is not our business, and the sooner we get out of the country, the better!"

Toria put down her cup and stared at him.

"Y-you said . . . 'we!' "

The Duke smiled.

"I am coming with you. I have something very precious which I have no desire to lose to a lot of rowdy peasants."

She saw then that he had a rolled-up bundle under his arm which she guessed were the pictures at which he had been looking when she first arrived.

She had put on her cloak before she came downstairs, and the Duke looked at her critically.

"You are too smart," he said. "Take off that cloak!"

Toria obeyed him, and he then had a rapid conversation with the man-servant, much of which she was unable to understand.

However, it was obvious that the man-servant did, and he went off towards the kitchen, taking her cloak with him.

When he came back he was carrying a very old and somewhat dilapidated coat of the type worn by peasant women all over the Balkans.

"Put that on!" the Duke commanded. "And take the chiffon off your head."

Without arguing, Toria did as she was told. He then produced a silk handkerchief of the type some men wore around their necks in place of a tie.

She put it over her head and tied it under her chin. As she did so, she caught a glimpse of herself in one of the mirrors on the wall.

She thought she would pass for a poor and very ordinary woman.

The Duke was wearing as an overcoat an ancient mackintosh such as a man might wear if he was fishing in the sea.

She guessed it was the same one she had seen him wear when he had stepped off the cargo-boat on his arrival.

Now he was giving some money to the manservant, who was obviously delighted at what he received.

He then opened the front-door, peering surreptitiously up and down the road before he said to the Duke:

"There is no one about. Go now, and God go with you."

"We shall certainly need His help," the Duke replied.

They walked out, and Toria realised it was very early in the morning.

The flag was not yet flying over the British Consulate and the streets were deserted.

Dawn had just broken, but there was no sun in the sky and there were lights in some of the windows of the houses they passed.

The Duke walked quickly, and moving beside him, Toria thought it would be a mistake to speak.

Besides, as his legs were far longer than hers, she had to exert herself to keep up with him.

He obviously knew the quickest way to the Port.

They went down several unimportant but residential streets before they came to the busier part of the City.

There, instead of the people hurrying to work, as they would ordinarily be doing, Toria saw there were little groups of people standing on the street corners.

They were talking and gesticulating to each other.

She could understand why the Duke thought it imperative not to go near them, and to keep as much as possible out of sight.

The streets twisted and turned, and always there were people standing about in groups, with men talking instead of working.

They did not, however, sound particularly aggressive.

At last they reached the Port, and Toria could see the Quay at which she had landed.

There was no sign now of the battleship which had brought her here from Naples.

Nor was there a sign of any ships, except for some small cargo-boats, and there were only a few of them.

With what Toria thought was a stroke of genius, the Duke found the man who was apparently in charge of the shipping.

Because she was feeling anxious, Toria did not listen to the long conversation they were holding.

Finally, in a somewhat resigned voice the Duke said to her:

"Come along. There is a cargo-boat leaving in about an hour's time, and we will be lucky if they will take us aboard."

Led by the man in charge, who was more attentive since Toria had seen the Duke passing him some money, they walked to the very end of the Quay.

Here they saw one small, very dirty-looking cargo-boat which was taking on a pile of wood besides what appeared to be a large consignment of vegetables.

The Captain, who looked scruffy and unshaven, and certainly an unwashed Klaklovan, at first refused point-blank to take any passengers.

It was then that the Duke and the man with him began to argue until finally the

Captain of the cargo-boat capitulated.

He was given what looked to Toria to be a large amount of money in cash which he accepted, counting it slowly, as if to make sure he was not being cheated.

Then, as the man who had brought them to the ship left, all smiles, with a few more bank-notes in his hand, the Captain told Toria and the Duke to come aboard.

He told them they could stay on deck or go below until the cargo had finished being loaded.

He, however, had no idea when that would be.

Because Toria was afraid of being seen, she suggested to the Duke that they should go below.

She was thinking that by this time those at the Palace would be aware that she was missing.

There would be a great commotion to find out what had happened to her.

"I shall feel safer if I am out of sight," she said to the Duke.

"You cannot anticipate that anyone would look for you here!" the Duke expostulated.

"I . . . I would rather go below."

"Very well," he agreed.

They went down the rickety companionway, the Duke following the directions he had been given by the Captain.

There were only two cabins — one of which was the Captain's, which Toria guessed would be as dirty as himself.

The other cabin was not being used except that a large piece of machinery had been put there, presumably to be carried to another Port.

There was one bunk, made of wood, with a mattress so torn and dirty that the floor, which was thick with dust, seemed cleaner.

There was the smell of oil and onions and, of course, of dirt.

But to Toria it was a place of safety from the King, and even Hell itself was preferable to becoming his wife.

"This is hardly the sort of place one would choose to be in," the Duke remarked sarcastically. "At the same time, I have no wish to be mixed up in the petty politics of a City that has no wish to accept an Englishwoman as their Queen."

"N-not . . . of course not," Toria murmured, "and at least no-one will see us here."

The Duke put his pictures down on the bunk, and on the floor a bag he had been carrying.

"As a precaution," he said, "I have

151

brought some food and a bottle of wine. I feel that anything they give us to eat on this ship will undoubtedly poison us!"

"I am sure it would," Toria agreed, "and it was very clever of you to think of it."

"I am not prepared to stay here," the Duke said. "I intend to go up on deck and see what is happening."

Toria gave a cry.

"You will not . . . go ashore so that they . . . move off without you?"

He smiled.

"I promise you they will not do that. Now, sit down, if you can find anywhere clean to do so, and remember, we shall have to spend quite a number of hours in this hell-hole. But there is nothing we can do about it!"

"I think it is a mistake to be so rude about it in case it takes umbrage!" Toria replied.

The Duke laughed.

"Then, of course, I must be more polite, and keep reminding myself that this is our life-line away from what will undoubtedly be a very unpleasant storm in the City."

Toria shivered.

The people might be rebelling against their English Queen.

But they had no idea that the English

girl in question had already made her escape from the horror and disgust she had felt for their King.

As the Duke left the cabin, Toria was praying fervently.

"Please, God, do not let them find me. Please, let me be safe in this ship until it leaves Klaklov . . . please . . . please . . . !"

chapter six

Toria hoped that the ship would leave at once, but she was too optimistic.

There was still the noise of cargo being carried aboard and men shouting to each other.

After a while she began to realise that the Duke was restless.

"When do you think we will leave?" she asked.

He had opened the port-hole and was standing looking out at the sea which was comparatively calm.

"I have no idea," he replied, "but at least you are concealed from whoever is frightening you."

Toria gave a little tremor.

She knew that by this time the Palace would be in an uproar at her disappearance.

There was always the chance that they would search the ships in the Port.

Because she was frightened, she said:

"Please find out when we are likely to leave."

"Very well," the Duke said, "but lock the

door when I have left, and do not open it until I return."

It was not a very strong lock, but she turned the key and heard his footsteps going up the companionway.

It seemed to her a long time before he returned.

When he did so, she knew by the expression on his face that it was not good news.

"I am afraid we still have some time to wait," he said.

"But . . . why?" she asked.

"The men are bringing the last of the cargo on now," he said, "but the Captain says they have to have some time off to have a drink before they will take the ship out to sea."

"I thought," Toria said tentatively, "that there was unrest in the City."

"I could hear occasional gun-fire," the Duke replied, "but it may be just the citizens celebrating, and it is certainly quiet enough here."

Toria thought that was not surprising, considering there were so few other ships in the Port.

For the next hour or so there was silence.

Then there was the noise of the Seamen coming aboard.

From the way they were talking and the

noise they were making, she guessed that some of them had had too much to drink.

Hoping to distract her attention, the Duke, while they were waiting, had unwrapped his pictures.

"I do not know if you know anything about Art," he said, "but I would like to show you what I have just bought, and which I find very interesting."

He spread them out on the bunk.

When Toria looked at them she gave an exclamation.

"I am sure that is a Poussin," she said.

The Duke looked at her in surprise.

"Do you recognise it?" he asked.

"Where have you seen a Poussin before?"

Because she thought it a mistake to say "In Hampton Court Palace," Toria answered:

"I have seen a reproduction of his *Gathering of the Ashes of Pancio*' which is in the collection of the Earl of Derby."

She saw the astonishment on the Duke's face and added quickly:

"My Mother is very interested in pictures, and we often talk about them."

The Duke did not say anything, but instead asked:

"And what do you think of this one?"

"I think it is lovely," Toria replied, "and he has expressed in it the profound thoughts for which I believe he was famous."

She was looking at the pictures as she spoke and did not realise that the Duke could hardly believe what he was hearing.

After a moment he pulled forward the painting by Morales and said:

"What do you think of this one?"

Toria looked at the exquisite picture, *"The Madonna and Child,"* and thought she had never seen anything so lovely before.

Then, as if she realised that the Duke was waiting for an answer, she said:

"I am sure I have never seen any paintings by this Artist before, but I think, although I may be mistaken, that he is Spanish."

"How can you possibly know that?" the Duke asked in amazement.

"I think perhaps I just sensed it," Toria answered. "But what he has portrayed seems unique, and different from most other religious pictures."

"You are right," the Duke said. "Morales was called 'Divine' even in his lifetime. Unfortunately not many of his works have survived."

"Tell me more about him," Toria begged.

After that, time seemed to pass quickly

while the Duke explained to her the genius of all three Artists who had poured their own personality into their paintings.

After the Seamen came aboard, there was still some delay before finally the ship got under way.

It was then the Duke collected his pictures together and put them down safely in the corner of the cabin.

As he shut the port-hole, Toria was aware that the dust and dirt smelt very unpleasant without the fresh air.

There was fortunately a small toilet off the cabin, where the basin was broken and the tiles on the floor cracked.

But there was a can of cold water in which they could wash off the worst of the dust from their hands.

There was only one bunk, and Toria wondered, if they were to stay the night on board, where the Duke would sleep.

As if he were aware of what she was thinking, he said:

"I hope we shall arrive where I plan to disembark before it is dark. I do not fancy sleeping on the floor, and you do realise the bunk is intended for only one person."

Toria blushed.

"I feel I ought to offer it to you," she said, "but this is the only gown I have to wear."

The Duke laughed.

"Then, of course, we must be very careful of it."

"I have an . . . idea," Toria said, "if you will consider it."

"Tell me what it is," he invited her.

"If we both sit on the bunk, covering it with the coat I was wearing, we could at least rest, although it might be a little cramped."

Then, as if she felt he might think she was being very immodest in suggesting they should be so close, she blushed and said:

"Perhaps it is wrong of me to suggest such a thing, but the floor is filthy and there are no chairs."

"I think your suggestion is a sensible one," the Duke said. "Now, you get into the bunk first so that you are close against the wall and I will sit on the outside, just in case anyone interrupts us."

Because she was rather tired, Toria was glad to do what he told her.

She squeezed herself into the bunk against the wall, feeling it was a relief to stretch out her legs.

The Duke sat down beside her, and as the ship gained speed and began to roll slightly, she was glad that the Duke was on the outside rather than herself.

At first they talked.

The Duke told her stories about pictures in which he was interested, and found it surprising that she knew so much about the different Artists and their work.

He had no idea that because the house in Hampton Court Palace was so small, Toria spent every available moment admiring the beauty of the Palace itself and its pictures.

She loved the tall, elegant rooms, and her Mother encouraged her to appreciate the pictures, which she found very romantic.

They would spend hours looking up one Artist or another and reading about his personality, his life, and his work.

Toria had no idea the Duke was thinking it was the most surprising thing he had ever known to find a young woman who was so beautiful, a young woman who at the same time seemed to be as immersed in Art as he was himself.

Again it flashed through his mind that it might be a trick of some sort.

But there was no possible way she could have known of his interest until he had shown her the three pictures he had just acquired.

He knew too that even the most experienced teacher would have found it difficult to instruct her in all the knowledge she had.

It was something that must have developed and deepened over years.

The cargo-boat steamed steadily on.

They ate the food the Duke had brought with him, and drank the wine.

As it grew dark, the Duke began to think that it would be impossible for them to find the yacht until it was daylight.

The sun had set and the first evening star was twinkling overhead when they drew into the harbour where he had left his yacht.

"Stay here," the Duke said, "and I will try to find out where we are."

What he really meant was to find out if "*The Siren of the Sea*" was anywhere to be seen.

He went up on deck, but saw at once there was no sign of her in the small fishing-harbour.

This meant, he knew, that his Captain would have taken her a little way along the coast to a quiet bay, where the yacht would not attract attention.

He went back to Toria.

"I am afraid I have bad news," he said, "and the best thing we can do is to stay here in this cabin until it is daylight."

"Must we do that?" Toria asked.

"I cannot imagine there is an Hotel of any sort in this small fishing-village," the Duke replied, "and if there were, it would not be the right sort of place for you."

She did not question what he said, and he went on:

"In that case, we will be safer here and less likely to be observed, however unpleasant it may be."

"Then, of course, I will stay here, if you want me to," Toria said meekly.

The Duke went away and talked to the Captain.

He found out that the cargo was not to be removed from the ship until it was morning.

He then sent a Seaman to buy some food, and, if possible, a decent bottle of wine.

The result was not very exciting, but there was fresh food and some goat's cheese, which was at least edible.

When they had finished their repast by the light of one candle, the Duke said:

"Now I want you to go to sleep. We have to walk quite a long way in the morning, and I suggest we set off at dawn, before anyone notices us."

"You do not think they are likely to do so?" Toria said in a frightened voice.

"Beautiful women in smart gowns are not often seen in a fishing-village!" the Duke remarked.

Toria blushed at the compliment, and he thought she was very young and very unsophisticated.

"Make yourself as comfortable as you can," he said, "and after I have taken away the remains of the food, we must both try to sleep a little before we set out at daybreak."

When he had gone, Toria took off the jacket of her gown and laid it, because there was nowhere else, on the old fishing-coat which the Duke had left on the floor.

She also put her slippers beside it before she got back onto the bunk.

When the Duke returned, he brought with him a rough bolster which he had managed to borrow from the Captain.

"It is fairly clean," he said, "but I did not like the look of his pillows."

Toria laughed.

"We must be thankful for small mercies."

"That is what I was thinking," the Duke replied.

He then took off his coat and his shoes and came to sit down on the bunk.

163

He had opened the port-hole, and while the night air was fresh, it was not cold.

"Now, try to get some sleep," he admonished Toria, "or you may find the long walk to-morrow too tiring, in which case I will leave you by the roadside!"

"How could you be so cruel?" Toria asked. "And if you do, I shall steal your pictures and run away with them!"

"You know I would not allow you to do that!" the Duke laughed.

He settled himself rather gingerly on the bunk.

He was thinking that this was a strange adventure which none of his friends would believe.

Here he was, with one of the most beautiful girls he had ever seen, and behaving as if he were her father or her brother.

He was aware that after her experience with the man who had frightened her, Toria was treating him as if he were a hundred years old.

He blew out the candle, and now there was the faint glow of the stars as they filled the sky overhead.

They were both silent, and after a little while the Duke was aware that Toria had fallen asleep.

He could hear her soft, even breathing.

Then unexpectedly she turned towards him and her head was resting on his shoulder.

Instinctively his arm went round her and she cuddled closer to him.

He knew she was completely unconscious of where she was.

It was then he became aware of the smell of violets.

At first he could not name the scent, but it gave her hair a freshness which he found very attractive.

He was not to know that Princess Beatrice had given Toria a bottle of perfume from a famous shop in Jermyn Street where Prince Philimon bought it for her because it was his favourite fragrance.

'If I were an Artist,' the Duke thought, 'I would paint a picture of Toria and me together as we are now.'

Toria awoke with a start and realised she was alone.

For a moment she was frightened, then the door opened and the Duke came into the cabin.

He was carrying a tray on which there were two cups of black coffee.

He set it down on the floor by the bunk.

"Now, hurry up," he said. "I am sure you do not want to stay in this dirty place one minute longer than you have to."

"I can hardly believe that I have slept so peacefully!" Toria said.

"There is nothing more tiring than fear," the Duke said, "but, as I have already said, hurry now, because we must be off. I am going to thank the Captain, and when I come back I hope you will be ready to leave."

He drank most of the coffee in his cup and went from the cabin.

Toria got off the bunk, aware that her expensive gown had been crushed, but felt the creases would soon fall out when she moved about.

There was a cracked mirror over the broken basin, and she tidied her hair as best she could, knowing there was not time to brush and comb it.

When the Duke came back she was ready to leave, except that she had not put on the coat which she had taken in exchange for her velvet evening-cloak.

"Do we need to take this with us?" she asked, pulling it off the bunk where they had slept on it all night.

"Put it round your shoulders until we are out of the village," the Duke ordered. "I will leave my coat as a present for the next occupant of the cabin."

"I am sure he will be very grateful!" Toria smiled.

They walked up on deck and Toria was relieved to see there were only two or three sleepy-looking Seamen about, with no sign of the Captain.

The Duke hurried her down the gangway, and having passed through the village, they walked along a rough road which bordered the sea.

They walked quickly, Toria carrying the shawl which contained her belongings, but she had difficulty in keeping up with the Duke.

After they had gone some distance, the Duke said:

"Now you can throw away that disfiguring object with which you have covered yourself."

Toria let it drop from her shoulders.

Then, as the Duke would have walked on, she said:

"Could we not walk on the beach which I can see is sandy? The stones on the road are hurting my feet."

"Of course!" the Duke agreed. "I should have thought of it myself."

They went down a slight incline which led them to the beach.

Once there, Toria sat down on the sand

to remove her slippers.

Then, as she realised that the Duke was not looking at her but out to sea, she quickly also removed her stockings.

She had been very stupid, she thought, in hurrying away from the Palace, not to have worn a stronger pair of shoes instead of the slippers which matched her gown.

But in her hurry to escape from the King she had put on the first pair that came to hand.

Not only were the soles too thin for walking, but also the fit, as they were new for her trousseau, was rather tight.

As she stood up, the Duke turned round, and going to her side, took the slippers from her.

"I will carry them!" Toria said.

"I will put them in my pocket," he replied. "I am sure you are wise to walk bare-footed."

"The sand is soft," Toria said.

Then, a little nervously, she went on:

"You . . . you are not . . . shocked that I should . . . walk like this?"

"Not in the slightest," the Duke said. "I think, on the contrary, you are being very sensible, and we still have some way to go."

It was in fact a lot farther than he had anticipated.

Toria was beginning to get tired and hungry, and before rounding the corner of a cliff the Duke gave an exclamation of delight.

Just ahead of them was a bay, and anchored in the bay, as he had expected, was *"The Siren of the Sea."*

He had not told Toria what he was seeking.

At the sight of the great yacht, which seemed even bigger in the small bay than it would have done in a Port, Toria asked:

"Are we going to try and reach that yacht?"

"We are," the Duke affirmed, "and as it belongs to me, I hope you will be suitably impressed by it!"

"It . . . belongs to you?" Toria questioned in astonishment. "If that is so, why do you travel in those dirty cargo-ships?"

As she spoke, she remembered she had not told him she had seen him arrive in one.

Fortunately he did not seem to notice her slip.

"It is something I will explain to you later," he replied. "But now we must hurry as quickly as possible and have a very large and enjoyable breakfast."

It was then she suggested she should put on her slippers before they actually boarded the yacht, and the Duke took them from his pocket and gave them to her.

The Duke was confident that the Captain and the crew would, as usual, preserve his incognito until they were instructed to the contrary. They would address him, not as "Your Grace," but simply as "Sir."

Toria was naturally most impressed by the yacht and the way in which they were received.

First she was taken below into the most beautiful cabin she could ever have imagined.

The Duke had in fact on several occasions entertained on his yacht some of the most beautiful women in England.

He had discovered, however, that when he was looking for pictures, he preferred to travel alone.

Women were a distraction, and he had found from bitter experience that they were not interested in anything but himself as a man.

When he was not making love to them they were bored, and if the ship was moving, they were often sea-sick.

He wondered now, as he showed Toria into the pink cabin, then went to the one next door which was his own, whether this young woman whom he found extremely alluring would, once they were at sea, be a disappointment.

If the Duke was in a hurry to go to the Saloon, where he knew his breakfast was waiting, so was Toria.

She washed her hands and face, gave a few pats to her fair hair, then ran up the gangway.

She looked so lovely coming into the Saloon that the Duke thought she might be Persephone bringing the Spring to a world of darkness.

But there was something very human about the way she enjoyed every mouthful of the eggs and bacon and covered several pieces of toast thickly with golden butter and honey.

"Now I feel better!" she exclaimed with a little sigh as she sipped the delicious fragrant coffee which a steward had brought them.

"So do I," the Duke agreed, "and I hope we never again have to go so long without food, or sleep in such filth."

"You must not be rude about it," Toria said. "It was my escape from the most frightening experience I have ever had in my life, and also, if you had not come with me, you might have lost your pictures."

"Of course I am sincerely thankful that I

did so," the Duke said seriously.

Toria smiled at him.

"How could I have guessed," she said, "that you were bringing me to anything so beautiful as this wonderful yacht?"

She put down her cup.

"Please, may I see every inch of it, and especially the engines? I have always wanted to see the engines of a ship."

She thought of how it was something she would have liked to do when she was travelling in the battleship, but was too shy to suggest it.

"I shall be delighted to show you over '*The Siren of the Sea*' from bow to stern," the Duke said as he smiled, "but now I think you should rest."

"Are you saying that because it is a polite way of getting rid of me?" Toria asked.

The Duke shook his head.

"Not at all. I was thinking of you."

"Then I do not want to rest," she said. "I want to see the Aegean Sea and watch the waves and the sky and think how beautiful it would look if it were painted by Guardi."

The Duke laughed.

"In which case, we will think that together," he said. "Let us start with the Bridge, and you can see how the ship is navigated."

He thought secretly that she would soon grow bored with the yacht, as most women did, and want to talk about herself.

To his surprise, however, she found everything entrancing and asked the most intelligent questions both of himself and of the Captain.

He had, of course, no idea that she had spent a great deal of her childhood with her Father, who had loved sailing in his small boat round the island on which they had lived.

After she had found her "sea legs" at about the age of three, she had never been sea-sick again, however rough the sea might be.

They looked at everything, and when finally they went back to the Saloon, the Duke said:

"And now I am prepared to listen to any criticisms you may care to make."

Although he was quite sure there would be none, he was pleased when Toria said:

"I am sure you own the most beautiful ship in the world! And now we will explore the horizon ahead of this and the horizon ahead of that, and there is always another and that is the only way to learn about the reality of life."

The Duke looked at her in astonishment,

but she was looking out to sea, and after a moment she said:

"Most people have to travel in their minds, but you can travel in your own ship and that means that you will be like Elijah going up to Heaven in a fiery chariot, or like Apollo, driving his horses across the sky to bring light to everyone who sees him."

She spoke as if she were speaking to herself rather than to him.

The Duke thought again, as he had already thought a dozen times, that she was the most extraordinary and unpredictable young woman he could possibly imagine.

After a moment he said aloud:

"I do not believe you are real! I think I have dreamt you and, as I have said before, you have come from Olympus to bemuse us mere mortals."

Toria laughed softly before she replied:

"That is a lovely idea, and if you are going to leave me in Greece, then I shall have to think very seriously as to how I can travel to England."

"I have not said I was leaving you in Greece," the Duke contradicted.

"I know," Toria said, "but I must not be an encumbrance on you, and you must get rid of me the minute you feel I have become a bore."

"There is no hurry, now that we are safe, to make decisions," the Duke said.

He wondered if Toria was excited by the idea of staying with him.

But he could see by the expression in her eyes that she was still worried and apprehensive.

"What is upsetting you?" he asked. "After all, you have escaped from the mysterious man who you thought was menacing you. He can hardly catch up with you here."

Toria did not answer.

She was thinking of how it was only a question of time before Queen Victoria would be informed of what had happened.

Lord Rosebery would tell her Mother, and everybody concerned would, once she got back, inform her that she must return to Klaklov and do her duty.

'I cannot . . . I cannot go back!' she thought frantically.

She suddenly became aware that the Duke was watching her.

"Come here, Toria," he commanded.

He was sitting on one of the soft sofas which were upholstered in green to match the colour of the Saloon walls.

Obediently she walked towards him.

He put out his hand and drew her down beside him.

"Now, listen," he said quietly, "we have been through a very difficult time together. Surely you must know by this time that I am your friend and that I will help and support you, and you need no longer be afraid?"

He felt her fingers quiver in his as he went on:

"Now that we are by ourselves in the middle of the sea, tell me exactly what is wrong, then together, I feel certain, we can sweep the trouble away."

Toria gave a little sigh.

How wonderful it would be if she could tell him the truth.

Then she knew that because he was English and because he too would expect her to do her duty towards the Empire and the Queen, she could not.

She took her hand away from his and said deliberately lightly:

"You know there are no problems. You have magicked away all the goblins, and I am no longer afraid."

It was a lie, and the Duke was aware of it but did not say so.

He merely told himself that sooner or later he would find out the truth and it could not possibly be as bad as this pretty child seemed to think it was.

They ate a delicious dinner early, then the Duke insisted that Toria go to bed.

"If you are not tired, I am!" he said. "There is always to-morrow with lots of things to see. I have told my Captain to put in at a quiet bay so that we can sleep in peace and not be disturbed."

"As you say . . . there is always to-morrow," Toria said in a low voice. "But . . . I am so afraid that when I do . . . wake up I shall find all this is a dream."

"I promise you, the yacht will be here and so will I," the Duke said.

"Then I will go to bed," Toria agreed, "but I do not want to waste too much time in sleeping."

She gave him a shy little smile.

Then, as he heard her running down the companionway, he thought that nothing in his life had been as extraordinary as what had happened since his arrival in Klaklov.

He was very thankful that he had been able to bring away three such outstanding pictures.

Because he was a connoisseur, he could not help regretting those he had to leave too soon to obtain.

"Where could they have come from?" he

wondered, and remembered his Cousin Robert had said something about the Palace.

Was it possible that the King was selling his pictures unbeknown to his Statesmen and his Curator?

The idea was laughable.

But if it were not the King, and there was no particular reason why he should be short of money, then who was the owner of such wonderful pictures?

That was one problem he had to solve.

The other, and more urgent, was Toria.

She might have stepped out of a picture herself, painted by one of the great Masters like Morales.

'She is lovely!' the Duke thought. 'But how, being so beautiful, is it possible she has to earn her own living, above all as a Governess?'

He knew only too well that they were prey to any would-be seducer of women.

Governesses were very much alone in a "No-man's-land" between the Gentry and the Servants' Hall, and therefore "fair game" for any roué.

Wherever they worked they ran the risk of being seduced by the Master of the house, the oldest son, or some visiting "womaniser" who could not keep his hands off any attractive woman.

He could imagine no Lady in her senses engaging Toria to be Governess to her children if she had a husband.

He thought it likely that her unpleasant experience in Klaklov would be repeated and re-repeated wherever she worked.

"What the devil can I do about her?" he asked himself.

Then he was afraid of the answer.

As he walked down the companionway to his own cabin, he told himself again that everything that had happened had been extraordinary.

It was like some strange fairy-tale drama in which he was being hypnotised or mesmerised until he could no longer think clearly.

As he shut his cabin-door behind him, he was vividly aware that Toria was nearby.

They were not as close as last night, but, although she was unaware of it, he had held her in his arms and learnt that her hair was scented with violets.

chapter seven

They finished dinner, and as they did so, the Duke said:

"To-morrow we reach Athens."

Toria rose from the table and walked across the Saloon.

She thought that she had been living in a dream-world and now he had brought her back with a bump to reality.

She had found the voyage entrancing.

The yacht had travelled slowly and they had watched the porpoises playing in the water, and admired the distant mountains.

They had talked on every subject in the world.

She had never known a man who stimulated her mind so that she found herself saying things that she had no idea she knew.

And yet, they seemed logical and interesting.

They had also stopped at small Ports and had gone ashore.

To the Duke's astonishment, they had found in a tumble-down Church a picture which he realised was well-painted although he was not certain of the Artist.

180

He offered what he thought was a respectable sum to the Priest in charge, and the man almost burst into tears.

To him it was the answer to his prayers, for the money would pay for repairs to the Church and also help the many poor people in the village who were old, hungry, and neglected.

"Are you taking this picture away with you?" Toria asked.

She studied it very carefully before she said:

"Whoever painted this painted from his heart, and perhaps his soul, and every stroke has been made with love."

The Duke felt no-one else could have given him such an answer and so simply, without the slightest pretension.

"I am sure you are right," he said quietly, "and we will find an expert who I hope will confirm that we have found an exciting addition to my collection."

"Tell me about your collection," Toria begged.

The Duke, however, was reluctant to reveal who he was.

He had seen so often the greed and excitement in a woman's eyes, not because he was a man, but because he was a Duke.

He knew that to Toria he was just an

ordinary man who indeed had enough money to possess a yacht, but was otherwise of no particular importance in the world.

Her behaviour was still very impersonal when she was with him.

He could not help wondering if she found him at all attractive or merely thought of him as somebody with no relevance to her as a woman.

Now, as she walked out on deck and he followed her, he thought that no-one could be lovelier and no-one could in fact look more like the goddess he teased her as being.

She was wearing the chiffon gown which she had brought with her simply because it was light in weight.

But it was in fact very like the robes in which the Goddess Aphrodite was depicted.

As the starlight shimmered on her hair, the Duke thought she was so ethereal she might vanish at any minute.

Toria leaned against the railing, and as if to reassure himself, he went close to her.

She turned her face towards the stars.

"Could anything be more lovely?" she asked. "Perhaps when we reach Athens and civilisation, that will spoil it."

The Duke did not speak, and after a moment she said in a different voice:

"I expect you will want me to leave, as I suggested I should when we reach Greece."

"Is that what you want to do?" the Duke asked in his deep voice.

Toria drew in her breath.

She knew she would be frightened to be alone, even in Greece, and she still had to make the long journey to England.

"I asked you a question," the Duke said, interrupting her thoughts.

"N-no . . . of course not . . . I should love to . . . stay with you . . . but I expect you have . . . different places to visit . . . and will not . . . want me."

"I did not say so," the Duke answered.

Then, as she looked at him, he put his arms around her, saying:

"I want you — of course I want you! How can I lose you any more than I can lose the stars that are shining above us?"

He pulled her against him.

Before she could realise what was happening, his lips were on hers.

He kissed her gently, then as she did not struggle and he felt the softness and innocence of her lips, his kiss became more passionate.

He knew as he kissed her and went on

kissing her that she was different from any woman he had ever kissed before.

He felt she had in fact been sent to him from Olympus and was not human, but was Love itself, just as it was portrayed in his pictures but which he had never found anywhere else.

To Toria it was as if the skies had opened and the stars had fallen down into her breast.

She had never been kissed, and she had often wondered if it was as wonderful as the Poets who wrote about it said it was.

She had thought too that it was a part of what she heard in the sound of music.

Then, as the Duke drew her closer and his lips became more demanding, she felt an ecstasy that was unlike anything she had ever known before seep through her body.

It passed from her lips to his and carried them both up into the sky.

She knew then that this was love; the love she had dreamt of, the love she had prayed she would one day find.

It was so wonderful, so rapturous, that she instinctively surrendered herself so that her body melted into his.

He kissed her until it was an ecstasy almost too tender to be borne. Then he raised his head.

"I love you, my Darling!" he said. "I have loved you from the first moment I saw you, and now we will be married and you will be mine for ever!"

He would have kissed her again, but she asked in a soft, incoherent little voice:

"C-an we . . . really do that?"

"It is what we are going to do," the Duke said. "My precious, I have not told you before, but I am in fact the Duke of Cannuncliff, and you will be the most beautiful Duchess that has ever graced my family's name."

He felt Toria stiffen.

Then in the same frightened little voice he had heard when he first met her, she asked:

"Wh-what are you . . . saying? What are you . . . telling me? Your name is Cliff!"

"That is my family name and the name I travel under," the Duke explained. "Otherwise everything I want to buy is doubled in price."

"Then . . . you really *are* a Duke?"

"Yes, I really am," the Duke said as he smiled.

Toria began to cry.

"No!" she said. "No, no, no! How can you be? And now I cannot . . . marry you . . . of course I cannot! Oh . . . how can this have happened?"

The Duke stared at her in astonishment.

Then, as the tears overflowed and fell down her cheeks, Toria turned and ran away from him.

She disappeared from the deck, and he knew she was running down the companionway to her cabin.

For a moment he was too nonplussed to move.

He had never dreamt, he never imagined, that any woman to whom he proposed would not have been delighted at discovering he was a Duke.

He knew before he left London that he had evaded every trick, every pressure to get married that had ever been thought of or written about.

It was not only the ambitious Mamas with *débutante* daughters who pursued him.

It was the widows, and even married Beauties who were prepared to accept the ignominy of divorce if it meant they could then become his Duchess.

And yet this girl, who had come to Klaklov to be a Governess, was horrified at the idea of his title and was refusing to marry him because of it.

"I do not understand," the Duke said to himself.

He walked down the deck and resolutely went below.

He knew Toria would be in her cabin, and without knocking he opened the door and went in.

The light that had been left burning showed him that she was lying on the bed, her face buried in the pillow, and she was crying tempestuously.

He shut the cabin-door and, crossing the cabin, sat down on the mattress.

"What has upset you, my Darling?" he asked. "It is not like you to cry like this!"

Toria did not answer.

Her whole body was racked with her tears.

"You were brave enough to escape from what frightened you," the Duke went on, "you were brave enough to travel with me in that dirty, foul-smelling cargo-boat, and you have not been afraid to be here in the yacht with me alone without a chaperone."

He paused before he said very quietly:

"Tell me — what is upsetting you now."

Still Toria did not speak, and after a moment he said:

"I thought when I kissed you just now that perhaps you loved me a little."

"I . . . I *do* love you," Toria sobbed brokenly, "I love you . . . with all my heart . . . and . . . with all my . . . s-soul."

Her voice broke before she went on:

"I have been praying . . . praying that you would love . . . me a little."

"I love you much more than a little," the Duke said gently, "and I cannot think of any reason why you should not marry me."

She did not answer, and very gently he put out his hands and turned her over until she was lying on her back, looking up at him.

Her cheeks were wet with tears, and she looked very tragic, but at the same time so lovely that he thought it impossible that anyone could be so beautiful.

"I love and adore you, my precious," he said. "Now tell me why you will not marry me."

Toria made a helpless little gesture with her hands.

She reached out to hold on to him as if she felt he would give her strength.

"I . . . I thought," she whispered in a hesitating little voice, "that you were just Mr. Cliff and if you . . . ever did anything so . . . wonderful as to . . . want to marry me . . . we could live quite quietly in a dear little house . . . and no-one would know . . ."

"Know — what?" the Duke asked.

He waited, and as Toria did not speak, he said:

"You must tell me, my Darling, what you

have done that makes it impossible for you to marry me because I am a Duke."

There were fresh tears in Toria's eyes.

Then, as they rolled slowly down her cheeks one by one, she said:

"I-if I tell you . . . you will perhaps not . . . love me any more so . . . please . . . will you kiss me . . . just once more?"

"It will not be just once," the Duke said firmly. "I will kiss you, as I intend to kiss you, all the rest of our lives together."

He put his arms round her as he spoke, and, bending over, took her lips captive.

He kissed her differently from the way he had kissed her before, and she knew that he was fighting her with kisses.

They were passionate, demanding kisses, and fierce, as if he were afraid he would lose her.

Only when they were both breathless did the Duke release Toria and sit up.

Surprisingly, he walked round to the other side of the bed and, lying down on it, pulled her against him.

As her head rested against his shoulder he said:

"Now, tell me what you have been concealing ever since I first met you."

He kissed her forehead before he added:

"If you have committed a murder or

stolen the Crown Jewels, I shall still love you, and about that there is no argument."

He felt Toria move a little closer to him, and because he knew what she wanted without saying so, he took the handkerchief from the pocket of his evening-coat and handed it to her.

She wiped her face, then put her head back against his shoulder.

He kissed her hair as he said very softly:

"I am waiting!"

"I . . . I am Princess Aleris!" Toria faltered.

The Duke was still.

"Princess Aleris?" he repeated. "Who was to marry King Inged?"

"I knew you would be . . . shocked," Toria said despairingly, "just as Queen Victoria and Lord Rosebery will be furious with me and will make me go back to him . . . but I cannot marry him . . . I cannot! He is . . . h-horrible . . . despicable . . . beastly . . .and so I . . . ran away."

The Duke's arms tightened.

"You ran away," he said, "and I promise you, you are safe with me. Now, tell me all about it."

"I . . . I am not . . . safe," Toria said in a pathetic little voice. "I thought if I stayed with you . . . no-one would be interested in

'Mrs. Cliff' . . . but how could you hide me if I were . . . your wife . . . and anyway . . . like the rest of the English, you will think it my . . . duty to save Klaklov."

"I think nothing of the sort!" the Duke declared. "What I do think, and this is the truth, is that you are mine and part of me, as we were meant to be since the beginning of time."

Toria looked up at him.

"Do you . . . really think that?"

"I swear it!" the Duke said. "Nobody, however important, shall take you from me."

Toria stared up at him as if she had to be certain he was speaking the truth.

Then she gave a little cry.

Hiding her face against his neck, she said:

"You saved me . . . and perhaps you can hide me . . . somewhere where nobody will . . . ever know where I am . . . and I can be with you and . . . love you."

"You will stay with me as my wife!" the Duke said firmly. "Now, tell me, my Darling, what exactly happened, and how having reached Klaklov — I think now it was the same day that I arrived in the City — you knew that after all that had been planned you could not marry the King."

Hesitatingly, because she was shy, Toria told him how hastily her marriage had been arranged and how even when her Mother slipped a disc in her spine Lord Rosebery still insisted the plan should go ahead.

"You must have had some idea there was opposition to the King," the Duke said, "and that the people in the City were dissatisfied with him."

Toria continued by explaining how strangely he had behaved when she arrived, how he had hardly spoken to her, but just sat, staring ahead.

Then, so softly that he had difficulty in hearing what she said, she explained how she thought she must speak to the King before the actual Wedding Ceremony took place.

She said how she had gone to his room.

As she told the Duke what had happened there, she hid her face against him and he could feel her whole body trembling.

When she ceased speaking he held her very tightly.

"And so you ran away," he said. "That was very, very brave of you!"

"I had seen you stepping ashore as I arrived in the battleship," Toria said, "and since I was sure that you were English, I asked one of the *Aides-de-Camp* to find out what was your name."

"I realised that some sort of ceremony was taking place on the Quay," the Duke admitted, "but I was not particularly interested, and only eager to get to my Cousin's house and see the pictures about which he had told me."

"I kept thinking about you," Toria whispered, "and I think . . . really . . . I fell in love with you . . . the moment I . . . saw you."

"Just as I fell in love with you," the Duke said. "When you came into the Sitting-Room I thought you were the loveliest person I had ever seen!"

"Oh, Darling, did you . . . really think that?" Toria whispered.

"Like you, I loved you from the very moment I set eyes on you," the Duke replied, "and because we were meant for each other, nothing shall divide us."

"But . . . you cannot marry me . . . you cannot!" Toria cried. "You know how . . . angry Queen Victoria will be . . . because I have upset her plans. She may turn Mama out of our . . . Grace and Favour house . . . and . . . we have no money."

"That is immaterial," the Duke said.

"What is important is that we have to make the Queen and everybody else realise that you could not marry a drug addict."

He felt Toria shiver.

"Forget him!" he said. "He is of no importance to us, and all that matters is our love."

He kissed her until her heart was beating as frantically as his.

Only when finally he left her so that she could sleep did Toria feel that, wonderful though it was, they were living in a "Fool's Paradise."

How could she possibly marry the Duke of Cannuncliff and ruin his life?

Even though they loved each other with their hearts and souls, he had his position to think of.

He had a family who looked up to him and he had his duty towards his Queen and country.

'I shall have to leave him,' she thought despairingly, 'or perhaps I could live in some remote little village where he could visit me sometimes.'

Then she knew it was an impossible dream.

Before she fell asleep from sheer exhaustion she thought perhaps the only solution would be if she could die.

At the same time, she wanted to live; she wanted to be with the Duke, she wanted to pour out her love for him.

And perhaps one day, if God blessed them, she could give him a son like himself.

"Oh, help me . . . help me," she prayed to her Father, knowing he would understand, having loved her Mother as he had never loved anyone else.

Although he had tried to reassure Toria, the Duke in the darkness of his own cabin was wondering desperately what he could do.

He could understand now all too clearly why the marriage arranged by Queen Victoria should have had to take place so hurriedly.

If there was dissatisfaction. among the people of Klaklov and some revolutionaries in the crowd assembling for the wedding, the reason for haste was obvious.

He remembered the sound of gun-fire he had heard during the night.

Although he had not worried Toria with it, the man-servant and his wife when he had spoken to them about it had been very voluble.

They had warned him of the dangerous

situation arising from the opposition to the Royal Wedding.

"Thank God I got her away!" the Duke said to himself.

At the same time, he did not underestimate the difficulties ahead.

Then something determined and strong rose up within him to make him certain that whatever happened, he would never give up Toria.

If the Devil himself tried to prevent it, he would still make her his wife.

Because he found it impossible to sleep, he rose as soon as it was dawn, and when he was dressed knocked gently on the door of Toria's cabin.

He did not wait for her to answer, but opened it.

She was not asleep, but had pulled back the curtains over the port-hole so that she could look at the golden globe rising in the sky outside.

The first rays of the sun were falling on her hair, making it seem to the Duke like a halo.

She looked like one of the Saints or an Angel in the pictures he had bought for his collection.

For a moment Toria did not realise he was there.

Then, when she did, she made a sound of sheer happiness and held out her arms.

The Duke moved to the bed and without speaking kissed her until it seemed to them both that they had become part of the sunshine now pouring into the cabin.

"I . . . I was dreaming of you," Toria said.

"And I have been thinking about you all night," the Duke admitted. "I am going now to tell the Captain to put into the next Port, where I will go ashore and find out what has been happening in Klaklov."

"You will . . . not let anyone know I am here?" Toria asked in a frightened voice.

"You will be quite safe until I return," the Duke assured her. "Do not hurry to get up, but just pray, my Darling, that nothing will turn out as bad as we fear it may be."

"They will be . . . looking for me," Toria whispered.

"But they will not find you," the Duke answered. "The world is a big place, and we will find hiding-places where we will be together."

"If only that could be true!"

"It can be," the Duke said reassuringly.

He kissed her again.

Then, as if he forced himself to leave her, he walked towards the door.

"Just pray and believe that God is mer-ciful," he said.

Then he was gone.

Toria prayed for a very long time before she got up and dressed.

She could not help a little pang of regret for all the beautiful gowns her Mother had chosen for her and which she had to leave behind in the Palace.

She thought too of the glittering wedding-gown and the veil that was to cover her face and shoulders, and shuddered.

She was sure that God had guided her when she had escaped from the Palace and slipped out through the gates without the sentries on duty noticing her.

She was sure that it was God who had taken her to the man she had thought of as "Terence Cliff" and whom she now loved with her whole being.

"I love him . . . I love him!" she said over and over again.

She thought, as she had last night, that it would be impossible to go on living without him.

She had breakfast in her cabin and, al-though she longed to go up on deck and await the Duke's return, she was afraid to do so in case somebody on the Quay should recognise her.

It would be a million-to-one chance against such a thing happening.

And yet if there was a hue and cry for Princess Aleris, who had disappeared from Klaklov, perhaps her picture was already appearing in the newspapers.

Then someone might become suspicious, if the yacht was known to have been anywhere near Klaklov, that the Duke was harbouring her.

As all this passed through her mind she told herself she must be very, very careful.

She sat in her cabin for a while, then went into the Duke's cabin because it made her feel nearer to him.

Tenderly she touched the hair-brushes he used, then she kissed the pillow on which his head had rested last night.

When there was still no sign of him returning, she began to grow frightened.

What could have happened to him? What could have occurred?

Was he at this very moment being cross-examined because he had been in Klaklov?

Suddenly she heard his footsteps coming down the companionway and jumped to her feet.

The door of his cabin was open and he saw her at the same moment that she saw him.

As he entered the cabin she flung herself into his arms.

"I was frightened . . . I was frightened because you were . . . so long!" she cried. "Oh, Darling . . . is everything all right? They are not . . . looking for me? Tell me they are not looking for me!"

The Duke held her very close against him, and moving her farther into the cabin, shut the door behind him.

Then, as she looked up at him beseechingly, he said:

"We have won, my precious! We have won! Everything is all right!"

"H-how can it be?" Toria asked despairingly.

Because it was hot, the Duke pulled off the smart yachting-jacket he was wearing and flung it down on a chair.

Then he pulled her into his arms and they sat down on the bed.

"What has happened?" Toria asked.

The Duke paused for a moment, as if he were searching for the right words.

Then he said:

"I am afraid, my Darling, you will find yourself married to a hero, and I hope you will not mind!"

"A . . . hero?" Toria repeated. "B-but . . . how . . . where?"

The Duke's eyes were twinkling, and as she looked at him in astonishment, he said:

"To make everything simple and easy to understand, I have concocted a brilliant story to explain why you are here on my yacht."

"You have . . . told them I am . . . here?" Toria said in horror.

"I told them," the Duke replied.

"I . . . I do not understand."

He kissed her cheek gently.

"I know, my sweet," he said, "but when I learned that King Inged had been assassinated the night before his wedding, I knew what story I would tell to explain why you were still alive."

"The . . . the King has been . . . assassinated?" Toria murmured.

"The revolutionaries stormed the Palace, overpowered the guards, and killed him before anyone was aware of what was happening. Then they went looking for you."

"And . . . I had . . . run away!"

"On the contrary," the Duke corrected her, "you were in the Palace, but an Englishman who was staying in the City under the name of Terence Cliff realised that his countrywoman was in danger."

Toria was listening to him wide-eyed, and the Duke went on:

"He managed to get into the Palace and, by the mercy of God, spirited you out of it with only seconds to spare before the revolutionaries would have killed you."

There was a somewhat twisted smile on his lips as the Duke continued:

"We fled across the City, and with the greatest difficulty persuaded the Captain of a very unpleasant and dirty cargo-boat to carry us to safety."

He smiled at her before he said:

"And of course you know the end of the story."

"You told this to the Ambassador and he . . . believed you?"

"Of course he believed me," the Duke replied. "He even congratulated me on knowing instinctively that you were in danger, and having the brilliance and the bravery to save you."

He gave a short laugh before he said:

"I shall doubtless be decorated by the Queen when we arrive back in England, and only you, my precious Darling, will know that I am an imposter."

"You are not . . . you are not!" Toria cried. "You *did* save me. But . . . does this mean that I can now marry you?"

"Of course you must marry me," the Duke answered. "Can you imagine that

Her Majesty Queen Victoria would countenance anything else when you have already spent three nights with me, alone and without a chaperone?"

Toria laughed.

"I do not believe you are saying this!"

"It is true," the Duke said as he smiled. "I have no option but to offer for your hand in marriage."

He pulled her closer to him before he said:

"We are going to be married immediately, and since we do not want people staring at us, we will be married on the first little island we can find that has a Church and a Priest."

"Can we . . . really do that?" Toria enquired.

"It is what we are going to do," the Duke said. "Then, my Darling, we are sailing for England, but first we shall visit Venice because there are some pictures I want to show you there."

He kissed her gently on the cheek before he went on:

"Then we will go to Naples and finally Marseilles. There will be no hurry, so we might slip across to Northern Africa before we end up at Marseilles."

"I do not mind where we go . . . as long

as I am with you," Toria said passionately.

"You may be quite certain that I will be with you, and we will be very happy," the Duke said. "And from Marseilles we will visit Paris, where I intend to buy you the most beautiful trousseau any Duchess ever possessed. After that, if we have nothing better to do, we will go home."

Toria put her hands up to her cheeks.

"I am dreaming . . . I know I am dreaming!" she said.

"It is true — or, rather — it will be true. And of course, you will be very proud of your 'hero husband' who has saved you from some very nasty assassins!"

"I love you . . . I love you!" Toria cried. "And all that matters is that I shall not . . . hurt you if I . . . become your wife."

The Duke kissed her again, very gently, before he said:

"I have sent a telegram to the Queen, telling her what has occurred and also one to Lord Rosebery, asking him to tell your Mother that you are perfectly all right, but suffering from shock. So in the circumstances we will not be coming back to England until you are well enough to undertake such a long journey."

Toria laughed.

"You think of . . . everything!"

"I think of you," the Duke said, "and that is the only thing worth thinking about, except getting married."

As he spoke, Toria realised that the engines were warming up and the yacht was moving.

"We are going to be married!" she exclaimed. "But, my Darling, I have nothing to wear as your Bride."

"I have thought of that," the Duke said as he smiled, "and I want you to wear the gown you were wearing last night. I have bought a veil and an enormous amount of white flowers. One of my Seamen is very skilful at making a bouquet."

"How can you be so wonderful?" Toria asked with a little catch in her voice.

"That was just what I was going to say to you!" the Duke answered. "And, my Darling, I think it will be very romantic for us to be married in Greece, where the gods have been with us ever since we met, and now there is nothing left to frighten you or to prevent you from being happy."

"How could I be anything else when . . . I am with you?" Toria asked. "I love you . . . oh, Darling, Darling, my wonder-hero husband . . . I love you until the whole world, the sky and the sea is filled with nothing but love."

"That is just what I was thinking," the Duke answered.

Then he was kissing her again, kissing her until there was nothing but the sunshine and their love.

They had found each other.

About the Author

Barbara Cartland, the world's most famous romantic novelist, who was also an historian, playwright, lecturer, political speaker and television personality, wrote over 570 books and sold over six hundred and twenty million copies all over the world.

She also had many historical works published and wrote four autobiographies as well as the biographies of her mother and that of her brother, Ronald Cartland, who was the first Member of Parliament to be killed in the last war. This book has a preface by Sir Winston Churchill and has just been republished with an introduction by Sir Arthur Bryant.

Love at the Helm, a novel written with the help and inspiration of the late Earl Mountbatten of Burma, Great Uncle of His Royal Highness, The Prince of Wales, is being sold for the Mountbatten Memorial Trust.

She has broken the world record for the last sixteen years by writing an average of twenty-three books a year. In the *Guinness Book of World Records* she is listed as the world's top-selling author.

Miss Cartland in 1987 sang an Album of Love Songs with the Royal Philharmonic Orchestra.

In private life Barbara Cartland, who was a Dame of the Order of St. John of Jerusalem, Chairman of the St. John Council in Hertfordshire and Deputy President of the St. John Ambulance Brigade, has fought for better conditions and salaries for Midwives and Nurses.

She championed the cause for the Elderly in 1956 invoking a Government Enquiry into the "Housing Condition of Old People."

In 1962 she had the Law of England changed so that Local Authorities had to provide camps for their own Gypsies. This has meant that since then thousands and thousands of Gypsy children have been able to go to School, which they had never been able to do in the past, as their caravans were moved every twenty-four hours by the Police.

There are now fourteen camps in Hertfordshire and Barbara Cartland has her own Romany Gypsy Camp called Barbaraville by the Gypsies.

Her designs "Decorating with Love" are being sold all over the U.S.A. and the National Home Fashions League made her, in 1981, "Woman of Achievement."

She is unique in that she was one and two in the Dalton list of Best Sellers, and one week had four books in the top twenty.

Barbara Cartland's book *Getting Older, Growing Younger* has been published in Great Britain and the U.S.A. and her fifth cookery book, *The Romance of Food*, is now being used by the House of Commons.

In 1984 she received at Kennedy Airport America's Bishop Wright Air Industry Award for her contribution to the development of aviation. In 1931 she and two R.A.F. Officers thought of, and carried, the first aeroplane-towed glider airmail.

During the War she was Chief Lady Welfare Officer in Bedfordshire, looking after 20,000 Servicemen and -women. She thought of having a pool of Wedding Dresses at the War Office so a Service Bride could hire a gown for the day.

She bought 1,000 gowns without coupons for the A.T.S., the W.A.A.F.'s and the W.R.E.N.S. In 1945 Barbara Cartland received the Certificate of Merit from Eastern Command.

In 1964 Barbara Cartland founded the National Association for Health of which she is the President, as a front for all the

Health Stores and for any product made as alternative medicine.

This is now a £65 million turnover a year, with one-third going in export.

In January 1968 she received *La Médeille de Vermeil de la Ville de Paris*. This is the highest award to be given in France by the City of Paris. She has sold 25 million books in France.

In March 1988 Barbara Cartland was asked by the Indian Government to open their Health Resort outside Delhi. This is almost the largest Health Resort in the world.

Barbara Cartland was received with great enthusiasm by her fans, who feted her at a reception in the City, and she received the gift of an embossed plate from the Government.

Barbara Cartland was made a Dame of the Order of the British Empire in the 1991 New Year's Honours List by Her Majesty, The Queen, for her contribution to Literature and also for her years of work for the community.

Dame Barbara has now written the greatest number of books by a British author passing the 564 books written by John Creasey.

Awards

1945   Received Certificate of Merit, Eastern Command, for being Welfare Officer to 5,000 troops in Bedfordshire.

1953   Made a Commander of the Order of St. John of Jerusalem. Invested by H.R.H. The Duke of Gloucester at Buckingham Palace.

1972   Invested as Dame of Grace of the Order of St. John in London by The Lord Prior, Lord Cacia.

1981   Received "Achiever of the Year" from the National Home Furnishing Association in Colorado Springs, U.S.A. for her designs for wallpaper and fabrics.

1984   Received Bishop Wright Air Industry Award at Kennedy Airport, for inventing the aeroplane-towed Glider.

1988   Received from Monsieur Chirac, The Prime Minister, The Gold Medal of the City of Paris, at the Hotel de la Ville, Paris, for selling 25 million books and giving a lot of employment.

1991   Invested as Dame of the Order of The British Empire, by H.M. The Queen at Buckingham Palace for her contribution to Literature.

The employees of Thorndike Press hope you have enjoyed this Large Print book. All our Thorndike and Wheeler Large Print titles are designed for easy reading, and all our books are made to last. Other Thorndike Press Large Print books are available at your library, through selected bookstores, or directly from us.

For information about titles, please call:

(800) 223-1244

or visit our Web site at:

www.gale.com/thorndike
www.gale.com/wheeler

To share your comments, please write:

Publisher
Thorndike Press
295 Kennedy Memorial Drive
Waterville, ME   04901